W9-ANZ-155

DARK ANGEL

After the Dark

Books published by The Random House Ballantine Publishing Group are available at quantity discounts on bulk purchases for premium, educational, fund-raising, and special sales use. For details, please call 1-800-733-3000.

DARK ANGEL

After THE DARK

MAX ALLAN COLLINS

Based on the television series created by
James Cameron and Charles H. Eglee

BALLANTINE BOOKS • NEW YORK

Sale of this book without a front cover may be unauthorized. If this book is coverless, it may have been reported to the publisher as "unsold or destroyed" and neither the author nor the publisher may have received payment for it.

Dark Angel: After the Dark is a work of fiction. Names, places, and incidents either are a product of the author's imagination or are used fictitiously.

A Del Rey ® Book
Published by The Random House Ballantine Publishing Group
TM and Copyright © 2003 by Twentieth Century Fox Film Corporation

All rights reserved under International and Pan-American Copyright Conventions. Published in the United States by The Random House Ballantine Publishing Group, a division of Random House, Inc., New York, and simultaneously in Canada by Random House of Canada Limited, Toronto.

Del Rey is a registered trademark and the Del Rey colophon is a trademark of Random House, Inc.

www.delreydigital.com

ISBN 0-345-45184-8

Cover art and design by Redseal

Manufactured in the United States of America

First Edition: June 2003

OPM 10 9 8 7 6 5 4 3 2 1

For the Dark Angel fans,
who keep the Freak Nation flag flying.

MAC & MVC

ACKNOWLEDGMENTS

Once again, my frequent collaborator Matthew V. Clemens—with whom I've written numerous published short stories—helped me here immeasurably. A knowledgeable Dark Angel fan, Matt co-plotted this tale and created a detailed story treatment from which I could develop *After the Dark,* which completes the trilogy editor Steve Saffel kindly commissioned me to create.

Steve again provided consistently strong support, which included not just rounding up materials, but adding his own creative input.

I would like to thank the creators of Dark Angel, James Cameron and Charles Eglee, for allowing us to continue and complete key aspects of their continuity. Thanks as well to Dark Angel scribe Moira Kirland Dekker; Debbie Olshan of 20th Century Fox; Wendy Cheseborough of Lightstorm; and, at Ballantine Books, Gillian Berman, Colette Russen, and Colleen Lindsay.

We would like to thank the many Dark Angel fans who have shown us support by way of sales, correspondence, and lively Internet discussion. It is, frankly, intimidating holding the reins of a storytelling franchise so beloved by its fans, who often know so much more about Dark Angel than we do.

Matt, Steve, and I hope that Dark Angel enthusiasts will appreciate this resolution to certain salient elements of this epic and—we trust—ongoing saga.

"Love sickness needs a love cure."
—Chinese proverb

"Love hurts."
—Phil and Don

Chapter One
A COLD DAY IN HELL

MEANDER RIVER, ALBERTA
DECEMBER 18, 2021

Six months on the run.

Six months in small towns, big cities, motels, hotels, campsites, public parks, cohabiting with the riffraff, even the homeless, scrounging, surviving . . .

What a humiliating tenure this had been, in the post-Pulse ruins that was America, for a man of Ames White's abilities and sensibilities. But White was, if nothing else, a man able to endure difficulties, to overcome hardships, to shrug off adversities that would defeat even above-average specimens of mere humanity.

True, he was not particularly blessed with patience—that attribute had always eluded him. Nor was grace in the face of frustration his long suit; forbearance in the presence of mediocrity—not his forte. Nor was compassion a trait he considered worth cultivating. So in his lack of "sensitivity," he seemed—to the second- and third-rate minds he so often encountered—cruel, even cold.

But such (wrongly) perceived cruelty and coldness only bespoke a superiority of mind and spirit, the end result of thousands of years of selective breeding; and, as such, were part and parcel of his ability to prevail. Anyway, Ames White was free of most of these primitive "human" emotions, though admittedly vestiges remained. He had loved a woman, once; and he loved his son.

But that was family. Breeding. That was allowed, even encouraged.

And Ames White was possessed with a dark, wicked streak of humor. He could well appreciate the irony of a "cold" character like himself finding refuge in the bitterly frigid Dene Tha town of Meander River, Alberta, Canada.

Its population no larger than the Sunday crowd in a Seattle marketplace, Meander River had taken him about as far north as he could manage, short of renting a dogsled. The people who lived here were so removed from civilization that White wondered if these subhumans had even heard about the Pulse, let alone felt its repercussions.

The Meander River economy was based on barter, and the citizens had very little use for computers, which meant scant had changed here, after what had been a cataclysm to the nearby United States. When terrorists set off an electromagnetic pulse over the East Coast back in 2009, the USA had lost everything, a superpower instantly reduced to the status of Third World nation. To Meander River, the event was as trivial as an electrical outage in a thunderstorm.

Buried under a mound of snow measured in feet,

not inches, Meander River was the perfect vacation getaway for the person who didn't want to be found by persnickety types . . . NSA federal bosses, say, who might be annoyed that a certain agent had gone rogue; or the Familiars, White's breeding cult family, who might be ticked that one of their own had failed in every one of his mission objectives, and could merit a reprimand . . . the fatal kind.

If those were the kinds of people you needed a vacation from, then Meander River had much to offer. Not only was there the biting cold and daunting snow, Meander River was also over three hours from the nearest pre-Pulse landing strip, and a good twelve hours from Edmonton and a real airport. Those conditions did not make travel to this fugitive's frozen paradise a simple proposition, particularly only a week before Christmas when the average high for the day was still well below zero.

Meander River was also located in the middle of the Dene Tha Native Reserve. Back in the United States, such locales were called Indian Reservations, with the generally abominable conditions to be expected as the end result of a several-centuries-long government-sponsored genocidal undertaking.

Up here, conditions were at least slightly better, with a school, a firehouse, a general store, and maybe a hundred clapboard houses, all in decent enough shape. The area was neatly maintained, without the abandoned cars and paint-peeling buildings White knew were par for the course on U.S. reservations. Best of all, the Meander River racial makeup meant that White wore reverse camouflage—he was one of only four or five persons in the town without the dark red skin and flat, wide features of the Dene Tha—giving him the prime advantage of seeing pale-face trouble coming from a long ways off.

The Familiars were universally white, racial purity being one element of the breeding recipe that had been perfected over countless centuries. And, of course, the U.S. government, particularly the ironically dubbed black ops agencies, weren't exactly renowned for their Rainbow Coalition hiring practices. So, for the time being anyway, White felt—if not safe—prepared to meet any difficulty, in this tiny Canadian burg.

Of course, White's whiteness had its downside. Among this dusky population, he stuck out like a failed Manticore experiment—he wouldn't have looked any more out of place had he been that imbecilic Dog Boy or that psychotic Lizard Man. While this would make him easy for his pursuers to spot, over all he maintained a certain peace of mind knowing that anyone hunting him would likely be in the same Caucasian—or at least non-Native American—boat.

Even so, White would also be harder to spot now than half a year ago, when his picture was broadcast on every television in North America. His spiky brown hair had grown out and covered his ears, a neatly trimmed beard and mustache replacing his previously clean-shaven face, giving him a well-groomed mountain-man appearance; his piercing dark eyes remained his most identifiable feature. The parka somewhat masked his lithely muscular build;

but then, he had always looked slighter and less capable than he actually was.

He thought of himself as a mild-mannered Clark Kent, who could remove his glasses, strip off his attire, and reveal the über-man beneath. On the other hand, he had no need for glasses, with his keen Familiar-bred eyesight, and no one had ever accused him of being mild-mannered, or of having any manners at all, when it came right down to it.

When White had first arrived here four months ago, the former NSA agent rented a small blue house once owned by a schoolteacher who had taken a post in Calgary. With its two bedrooms, a sometimes functioning TV aerial, a bathroom with perpetually cold running water, and living-room fireplace, the one-story clapboard at least kept out the chill. He had enough money to live comfortably up here, the benefits of both government service and money provided him by the Familiars to run their operations.

Working for two secret organizations over half a decade had kept a steady flow of untraceable cash running through White's hands and flowing into numerous bank accounts under as many names. The fact that the NSA didn't know about the Familiars had allowed him to work both sides of the fence. For their part, the well-funded Familiars had been in existence longer than anyone could imagine, and they had wanted White to maintain his position within the NSA. The loss of that position through the treachery of his subordinate Otto Gottlieb would definitely have angered his Familiar superiors, a good reason for White to take this extended Canadian getaway.

Eventually, he would have to approach the Familiars and make peace with them, though doing so would surely mean risking his life. His priority for these many months had been survival—to retrench and use his best weapon . . . his mind . . . to begin working out a solution, to think his way out of this seeming impasse. He had personal desires, involving his boy, but he still shared the beliefs and goals of the Familiars, and his goal was to convince them that he should be allowed a second chance.

And yet still he remained in Meander River—telling himself that he was merely allowing the Familiars to cool off, to achieve a distance from his failures that might allow him to present his case before dispassionate judges. Truth be told, though, he had come to like living up here, where just getting by was a little harder—it gave him a feeling of tranquillity, and also pride that he was not only surviving, but adapting quite well to his new surroundings. He was free of the stress of his former double life. Someday, when he and his son Ray were reunited, this might be the sort of place where they could live together.

Even White's dreaded migraine headaches—something he struggled against constantly while working for the government (of course, those assholes could give Jesus Christ migraines)—hadn't bothered him nearly as much as he'd settled into life in Meander River. Pain was something White and those of his breed had largely overcome—their pain thresholds had been bred to near extinction, the remnants remaining only to serve as the warning system nature intended. But certain physiologically driven discomfort—genetically passed along—broke down the well-bred defenses of White and his kind . . . the migraines a prime example.

Bundling up in a parka, ski mask, and boots, White prepared for the short walk to Malcolm's, a combination restaurant and bar that was the only place in town to get either a hot meal or a real drink. Cooking not being among his many skills—and not an interest he wanted to cultivate—White spent a lot of time at Malcolm's, where the hired help, as well as the owner himself, had long since recognized him as a regular.

They were a stoic, sour bunch, however, still treating him like a stranger, an outsider. Perhaps it was racial, but in any event, White had the unmistakable feeling that none of the Malcolm's crew liked him. It wasn't an uncommon response on his part; people often appeared to instinctively feel an antipathy toward him, probably because of his well-earned air of superiority.

White didn't give a good goddamn whether these savages liked him or not, another common response on his part. If he could not be with his own kind—his son, for example—Ames White was quite content with his own company. If anything, he appreciated the staff at Malcolm's for not inflicting small talk upon him—such interaction was a part of life among the mongrel humans that he had endured far too long.

Trudging down the street, White once again considered all the things that had gone wrong in the past twelve months or so, and the people who had been responsible. At the top of this ignoble list was the transgenic bitch called Max—he had missed numerous

opportunities to either capture or kill the X5—specif-
ically, X5-452—who had turned his life into a living
hell. His faithless NSA partner Otto Gottlieb had not
only turned on him, but ratted him out to the only
enemy as dangerous as 452 herself: Eyes Only, the
underground cyberterrorist.

The rebel investigative journalist—whose identity
remained unknown—was always prying into matters
of importance; most of this interference had been pe-
ripheral . . . annoying but never anything that could
truly block White in his own sub-rosa efforts. That
had all changed, however, when Eyes Only broadcast
one of his trademark video hacks, the subject of
which was Ames White.

For all intents and purposes, the renegade broadcast
had ruined both of White's careers, tainting him not
only with the NSA but the Familiars. And Eyes
Only's little unscheduled "program" had even been
highlighted by segments showcasing inside information courtesy of that wimp NSA underling Sage
Thompson and White's own former partner, Otto.

And though this was the major setback that had
sent him scurrying for his life in the anonymity of
Meander River, even that could not compare to the
loss of his son, Ray. Kidnapped by 452 and an
unidentified man from the Familiar's own school,
Brookridge Academy, the boy was now MIA, leaving
no clues to his whereabouts. In the end, he not only
had lost Ray, but his wife Wendy as well.

Of course, White had killed Wendy himself . . . a
necessity, considering her treachery toward him; but
that didn't negate the nagging needle of loss. His wife

had been a fine companion, with many good quali-ties—she just hadn't known when to let things go. In the long run, though, he supposed he and Ray were better off without her—she was merely the vessel for Ray's creation and, as such, lacked the breeding he and his son shared.

The most important thing now was to find Ray. Someday, White knew, he would get his son back. But this was a search he dared not undertake until he'd made his peace with the Familiars.

And in a matter of days—and he did wish he could be with his brothers when it happened—an event would transpire that would put his people on the top of the world. He might seem more valuable to the Conclave, soon—when his expertise and knowledge of X5-452 would come in very handy . . .

Even on the best of days, as its name implied, Meander River wasn't exactly a bustling metropolis; but as White strode down the deserted street, it dawned on him that things were even more quiet than usual . . . and usual was pretty damned quiet. As snow blew through, on a moan of wind, like cold sand thrown in his face, White felt as though he were walk-ing through a snow-covered, subzero ghost town. His pistol nestled in the usual belt holster at the small of his back, the cold steel against his spine somehow re-assuring; and a second gun was snugged in his parka pocket, where he could get at it immediately. So there was no need for apprehension.

You've been in the boonies too long, he told him-self.

The snow crunching beneath his boots, the frigid

air carrying the not unpleasant aroma of Malcolm's beef stew, now barely a block away, White recalled the pre-Pulse homily: "Just because you're paranoid doesn't mean they're not out to get you."

But White's newly revised version was, "Just because they're out to get you doesn't mean you have to be paranoid." He smiled at the thought—even on the run he could maintain control—and started to cross the alley that ran beside Malcolm's.

And, as he did, from the alley emanated a deep voice—unthreatening, not at all loud, and yet booming: *"Fe'nos tol."*

White froze.

The familiar greeting of the Familiars.

After all these months . . . they had found him. Just because you're not paranoid, he thought, doesn't mean they won't get you. It didn't matter how they'd managed it, only that they were here, that they had somehow gotten into town without his being aware. He forced out a long, slow breath, a plume of cold steam rising from his mouth as he turned to face the voice.

"Fe'nos tol," he replied.

Two men faced him, each winter-bundled in parkas much like his. They also wore full ski masks, but whether these were men he would recognize, with their faces exposed, was a moot point. Who they were wasn't as important as who they represented.

It would seem the Familiars wanted him a lot more than he'd thought; so much for lying low till spring.

Still watching the two in front of him, White became aware that three more had materialized behind him. His skills, like those of his stalkers, were far above those of normal humans. White didn't need to see the three men behind him to know they were there—he felt them, his combat radar pinging away at his surroundings.

And yet they had surprised him—come up behind him on the otherwise deserted snowswept street without him tipping to it, till now. They were good—the Familiars had sent their best trackers after him. Somehow, he did not feel a warm rush from the compliment . . .

A thousand years of breeding by the Familiars had gone into making the strongest human beings possible, superhumans, actually. Only the man-made abominations of Manticore could hold a candle to the Familiars.

Without moving, giving them nothing physical to react to, White said, "From our ancestors. For our children's children."

The ski mask on his left replied, "From my father before me. For my sons."

Then both men pulled pistols from their pockets— small, silver guns with noise suppressors exaggerating the barrels.

So much for friendly greetings . . .

Keeping his gloved hands unthreateningly loose at his sides, clearly not in a position to go for a gun in a timely fashion, White plotted his next move. These were trackers, not assassins—oh, they would kill him if necessary, but had their mission been to kill him, the greeting would have been bullets, not words.

But there was no use trying to talk to them or reason with them or stall in any fashion. No one of these men was going to be swayed by words—even bribes would fall on deaf ears—and the truth was, he was outnumbered five to one.

Combat 101: when confronted by superior numbers—attack.

White took one swift step forward and leapt, his legs splaying wide as he kicked both men standing in front of him simultaneously. The one on the left grunted as White's boot struck him in the chest, the man's gun firing reflexively, the bullet sailing off across town trailed by the *snick* the gun made; the ski-masked tracker's feet went up and his head went down as he landed on his back in the snow with a faint *whump*. The one to White's right didn't even get out a grunt as White's boot caught him in the face, breaking his nose, dropping him to the snow, unconscious, gun dropping from his fingers, burying itself in a snow bank.

White landed nimbly, then swung a leg around, in such a blur of speed that even trained types like these could only back away awkwardly. At the end of his motion his leg hit the ground, and then he was running, down that alley, leaving the fallen two behind, the other three coming after him.

No shouts, no cries, from these pursuers—only their breath, barely audible behind him. Fast as he was, White had no hope of outrunning the trio—these were not ordinary men, but Familiars like himself. Still, with some luck, he might be able to pick a better place to make his stand.

It did surprise and encourage him that they weren't firing at him. They would have their guns in hand by now—he didn't look back—and that meant there were no exterminate-upon-resistance orders for these trackers.

He ran with long, easy strides, all those generations of breeding paying off, as he barely broke a sweat. Finally sneaking a look over his shoulder as he rounded a corner to his left, he could tell the three were still back there, the distance holding steady at about fifteen to twenty yards.

He took a right turn, then crouched in a doorway and waited; he did not arm himself, leaving both pistols packed away. As his mind raced, one dominant thought prevailed: *he did not want to use a gun on them!* Although his stock with the Conclave—the Familiars' governing body—was at an all-time low, killing a Brother would send White careening across a line from which there was no possible return, except in a body bag.

The first Familiar came around the corner, and White exploded out of the doorway to deliver a flying kick to the man's head, knocking him off his feet. The second one emerged just as White rolled and bounced to his feet. The Familiar attacked—like White, the man did not have a gun in hand—but White was ready. He dodged, he parried, and as the ski-masked assailant delivered one martial arts move after another, White avoided each, looking for an opening.

As the third man barreled around the corner, White saw his chance. Spinning away from number two, he delivered a side kick to the solar plexus of number three and knocked him on his ass, the man's breath jetting from him as if he'd expelled a small cloud.

Coming around to number two again, White executed a perfect leg sweep, dropping the man onto his back. Pressing the advantage, he caught the man across the clavicle with a quick chop and heard a sharp crack as the Familiar's collarbone snapped; but the man didn't cry out—pain wasn't an issue, really, but other physiological responses pertained, in this case unconsciousness.

He paused momentarily, considering his three fallen adversaries, none of whom had come after him with gun in hand. The Conclave clearly wanted him alive . . . and that was a good sign, wasn't it?

Wasn't it?

Answering himself with a shiver, White sprinted off in the direction he'd been going, then turned right at the next corner, his mind working on the next chess move, when another Familiar stepped from the recess of a darkened doorway, a Tazer in his right hand.

Questions fell like snow—where had *this* masked figure come from? How had the man gotten in front of him while he was fleeing? These thoughts and a dozen others flashed through White's mind in the moment it took the two darts to erupt from the end of the Tazer and puncture White's parka.

He felt two sharp pricks in his chest, then his limbs flapped uncontrollably, and his feet lost their purchase and he found himself on his back, looking up at the gunmetal-gray sky. All the antipain breeding of centuries could not stop the electrical storm in his body from having its way with him, his veins on fire as current circuited through him, the questions gone now as the sky turned charcoal and everything around him grew very quiet.

After only a few seconds, White surrendered to the unfamiliar sensation of extreme pain, and then it faded and he felt himself dropping away from Meander River, Alberta, as if he'd stepped off the edge of a cliff, plunking into an abyss, a place much colder than his Indian reservation refuge, and darker even than his darkest thoughts.

The first thing Ames White realized, even before he opened his eyes, was that his gun was gone. The cold steel, the almost happy discomfort of the pistol binding against his waistband, was absent—it was like realizing a pickpocket had taken your wallet. He reached back and confirmed the weapon's absence from his spine at the top of his slacks.

Despite what he'd experienced, White did not feel the ache, the soreness a typical human would experience; but he did feel an uncomfortable weakness, a certain leadenness, and the area in his chest where the darts had penetrated tingled, in an annoying, tickling fashion. This sensation immediately gave clarity to his thoughts and memory, and he remembered being found by the Familiars.

He was somewhat surprised to be alive, though the actions of the trackers had indicated the Familiars had ordered his capture, not liquidation. Whether or not this was a pleasant surprise remained to be seen . . .

Opening his eyes to dim illumination, White surveyed his surroundings and his situation. He was in a sparse gray cell, asprawl on a cold stone floor, the cell barren but for bars inset in a small window of the door—no bunk, no toilet; the cell was clean, the stinging smell of antiseptic tweaking his nostrils. A small, naked lightbulb hung in the hall beyond the tiny window, providing the only light; somewhere, water dripped. He still had his clothes (another surprise), but his parka, belt, and boots had been removed.

Looking into the hallway through the bars, he saw not a row of other cells, but a blank stone wall, where shadows danced and jumped. White knew that most ordinaries—the term both the Familiars and the transgenics used to refer to "normal" humans— would be paralyzed by fear to find themselves in such a dank, dark environment, and would constantly search the shadows for mice, rats, or something worse.

White, on the other hand, found the cell comforting. These surroundings, in and of themselves, presented no problems. His only concern now was coming up with a plan that would get him the hell out of here. No matter how bleak his future might appear, one favorable fact remained: the Familiars hadn't killed him immediately when they found him.

"You have failed repeatedly, Brother White."

The voice rattled the bars—a booming basso profundo, piped in from somewhere in the darkness of the cell ceiling.

White was startled, but only momentarily. Despite the obvious attempt at intimidation, this was not the voice of God, unless God had a German accent . . .

and, since that seemed unlikely to White, he had a good idea who among the Conclave was doing the talking.

"That's true," he answered, calmly.

"And you know the price of failure."

The voice had all the warmth of December in Meander River.

"I do. But—"

"But? *You're going to try to negotiate with us, at this point? . . . After these countless failures?"*

White had the good sense to not answer.

". . . Do you imagine you have something with which to negotiate?"

Despite the sarcastic tone, the man seemed to be *leading* him—as if trying to . . . help him?

Why?

White knew this man to be a key figure among the Conclave, wielding a power far greater than any he himself had ever hoped to achieve. And yet now, for some reason the former NSA agent could not comprehend, this important figure was trying to guide him in this dark hour.

White considered his response carefully—the correct answer could mean another chance for him, and the wrong answer . . . well, that would most assuredly lead to the imminent death he had expected ever since seeing those ski-masked trackers back in Meander River.

Injecting the proper confidence into his voice, Ames White said, "I can deliver X5-452."

At first silence . . .

. . . then a terrible, dismissive laugh rattled the speakers in the ceiling.

Chilled, White realized instantly that he had just made a tragic, perhaps even a fatal, error. His response did not seem to be what the Conclave figure had wanted to hear.

But what else could he offer them besides 452? Every plan for the future the Conclave had made hinged upon that bitch's extinction! Within days, the comet would arrive, and a new era would begin—an era threatened only by the existence of X5–452! What in hell could be of greater importance than "Max"?

A terror rose within him—a panic that urged him to scream, to beg for his life; yet some strength in him wisely prevented any sound, any words, from coming out. But the logical part of him, his keen intelligence, failed him as well—he simply did not know what to say, what to bargain with . . .

"You can 'deliver' X5–452—how many times have you promised us that very thing?"

"More than once, I know."

"And how many times has she bested you? How many times have you failed your brothers?"

"Too . . . too many."

"What makes you think this attempt will be successful? Why should this be any different from all the other failures?"

Hesitantly, White said, "The plan I have in mind is—"

"Foolproof? Like all of your other cunning plans? . . . You've had so many plans, haven't you,

Brother White . . . and yet on every single occasion she has defeated you."

"Meaning no disrespect," White said, "she has defeated us—all of us—too frequently. As much as we may despise her and what she represents, she is a worthy foe."

"Worthy . . . ?"

"If she were an insignificant impediment, her existence would not pose such a threat to our cause."

Now a terrible silence followed, and White wondered if he had spoken too frankly, if his brashness would result, finally, in the ultimate, fatal censure of the Conclave.

"Your previous 'plans' have left much to be desired, Brother. How can you reassure us of your abilities? How can you restore our faith in you?"

"You can allow me to present my plan to you. For your consideration. Surely I don't need to remind *you* that only *days* remain."

". . . Speak, then."

Taking a deep breath and letting it out slowly, forcing himself to stay calm—losing his temper here would be to lose his life—White explained the scheme, in broad but complete strokes. Even he didn't know every detail as yet, but the high points were already in place, and he went with them.

And, too, there were aspects of his plot that it was best the Conclave not know, at least as yet—not until after the ends had justified his means. The important thing for the Familiars at this moment was he could deliver to them 452 . . . and the Coming would remain securely on schedule.

"This plan will lead to the successful capture of X5-452?"

"I'm staking my life on it," White said.

"That much is guaranteed."

What followed wasn't exactly silence—a muffled whispering, as the voice above and other Conclave members discussed White's proposition.

And then: *"Do you have funds?"*

A hopeful sign.

"Yes," said White. "Some."

"Then those funds will finance the operation."

White couldn't stop himself, blurting, *"My own money?"*

The voice remained calm. *"Whatever funds you have are yours only by our dispensation."*

Best not to challenge that.

"Now that that is settled," the voice said, *"we'll turn to the timetable . . ."*

Rubbing his forehead, trying to stave off one of his headaches, White said, "We can start as soon as you see fit, sir . . . Might I ask to join you in better quarters, better circumstances?"

"You know you can't afford to fail again."

"I do indeed, sir."

"That should you fail, there will be no reprieve."

"Yes."

"Only your family's history with the Conclave allowed you to buy another opportunity this time."

"Thank you."

White remained stubbornly passive. He knew they were watching him from somewhere, knew too that they were well aware that he hated being lectured as much as he hated to fail. He would not give them the satisfaction of seeing him lose his composure.

Soon the sound of a key in the door announced his return to the Conclave fold as grandly as a fanfare of trumpets.

Forcing himself to breathe deeply and slowly, he instead concentrated on the jackhammer pounding in his skull. He was coming to understand that pain had its purposes, and in this case, it seemed to help him focus.

In the case of 452, her pain would bring him only pleasure, and her death would ensure the triumph of the Conclave, in the imminent Coming.

Chapter Two
NAUGHTY AND NICE

SEATTLE, WASHINGTON
DECEMBER 20, 2021

From the op ed page of the *New World Weekly*:

Sketchy's Sketchbook
by C.T. "Sketchy" Simon

"Silent Fright"

Not so long ago, if you'd told Emerald City residents that they'd see Christmas lights strung from the high fences of Terminal City, you'd have been not so politely told you were frickin' nuts.

But a lot has changed in the six months since the so-called "Terminal City Siege" began. For one thing, the siege is officially over—both the unconventional residents of the compound and city government agree on that point. Though a brace of police cars remains parked outside the gates, 24/7, the truce has held.

That truce was struck not long after the apprehension of Kelpy, the chameleonlike serial killer captured by the transgenics themselves—the one, defining action that had convinced many in the city that the Manticore refugees were serious about wanting nothing more than to fit in. The National Guard is long gone now, as is the threat of the U.S. Army.

Still, a large segment of the populace remains unconvinced, and so the police still stand guard at the gates. The new mission of the boys in blue, however, is to keep out those who would try to destroy the peace, and not pen the transgenics in.

The denizens of Terminal City are now considered Seattle citizens, American citizens, as equal as any other. Of course, that still doesn't sit well with some of our fine city's less understanding occupants. So, most of those who live inside Terminal City remain within the confines of this offbeat gated community, seldom venturing out for more than work.

Their new place in the community, however, has garnered the transgenics a controversial nonvoting seat on the city council, and at the next election, Terminal City will elect its own alderman to a regular city council post. The *New World Weekly* supports this decision—the transgenics are human beings, too, after all, even if they are genetically enhanced creations of a secret government operation gone awry. (*Editor's Note:* Elsewhere in this issue, read the latest article in our continuing Freak Nation series:

"Manticore—the U.S Government Freak Show
You Paid For!")

For the time being, Max Guevera—the enigmatic, beautiful, raven-haired X5 who negotiated the peace—remains the de facto mayor
of Terminal City. The dark-eyed and high-
cheekboned Max—whose full lips and pleasing
form draws stares from men and women alike—
has a sultry presence that allows her to succeed in
leading this rabble into becoming a full-fledged
community. Her taking a stand . . . her courage
and leadership . . . has been the backbone propping up this ragtag bunch of squatters since those
early difficult days of the siege.

In a black ensemble of turtleneck sweater and vest
and form-fitting slacks and boots, the petite, shapely
killing machine that was Max Guevera sat in a booth
in a restaurant across the way from Terminal City. She
was sipping coffee, reading the tabloid rag her friend
Sketchy wrote for, a half smile dimpling one cheek.
Oblivious to her own Catwoman chic, Max shook her
head, thinking she'd have to give Sketch a little kick
in the behind for that "sultry presence" stuff.

Ironic, though, that of all the media, the sleazy *New
World Weekly* would become the voice of reason, the
first among the press to take the side of the transgenics. Ironic, too, that this least respected of Seattle
publications would be the only one with national impact, due to its grocery store checkout-counter status
across America.

Other than her own centerfoldish write-up, she

could hardly argue with anything Sketchy said in his editorial. Things were better for the transgenics now—surprisingly so, considering the genocidal threat they had faced. Still, problems remained—different problems, new ones, often mundane—and a peacetime Max found herself having difficulty adjusting to such minor troubles in a way the wartime Max had never experienced, where major troubles had abounded.

Being bred as a genetically enhanced super soldier had its advantages, no question; but as much as Max had complained about wanting to fit in—and to be like everyone else, and just live in peace—there'd been too many times during the last six months when she felt a restlessness, a yearning for action that distressed her. Had Manticore hardwired her in a way that meant a normal life would remain out of reach, despite her best efforts?

These thoughts, these feelings, troubled her, especially since everything seemed to be falling in place for her fellow transgenics.

Incursions by antitransgenic forces had been nil—unless you counted the occasional protesters—and, for their part, the Manticore refugees were fitting in nicely with the community, economically if not physically. To their surprise, the same attributes that made them premium-quality soldiers had also served them well in a business setting. With handsome X5 Alec leading the way through much of this new wilderness called commerce—had he been an '80s yuppie in a former life?—the transgenics had not only become successful, but were actually thriving.

The spark for this pleasant bonfire of capitalism in the transgenic commune had been an unlikely one. It turned out that the very first Manticore creation—that hulking, lovable dog boy, Joshua—wasn't the only Terminal City resident with an artistic bent. Joshua's paintings had earned him money before, in a top Seattle gallery, and with the group in need, he'd painted with a new fervor.

Based upon his sheer, instinctive talent, Joshua had been successful even before his tabloid celebrity, and now the value of his powerful, primitive paintings was skyrocketing. Gallery owners were clamoring for more "transgenic art," and the residents of Terminal City responded.

Dix, the potato-headed security man with the monocle, and his baseball-skulled partner Luke, were more than engineering whizzes who had hooked up Terminal City's security network, supervised the motor pool, designed and built its own power generator and water system. They were also burgeoning welding sculptors, forming abstract shapes that created concrete images in the eyes and minds of viewers. Overnight their hobby became a business.

And Mole, it turned out, had a knack for sand sculptures; and many of the others had skills of their own, not always on the artistic level of Joshua and the sculptors, but in an arts-and-crafts fashion reflecting their own peculiar makeup.

Max grinned at that thought. Let's face it, she told herself, who on this planet has a more unique combo of environment and genetics in their past than the transies?

So they opened up a street market, and within a month the transgenic art had become a hit with patrons throughout the city, from culture mavens to average folks. Not only were the transgenic artisans prolific, they were talented, *and* they were media darlings—not the first media devils who'd made that transition—whose pieces fetched top dollar. In less than three months they had leased the seven-story building on the corner across the street from the main gate.

To Max, the seven-story home of Terminal City Artworks was a building with memories. It had been in the coffee shop on the first floor of this building that she and Detective Ramon Clemente began to finally share the truth with each other—in the critical Kelpy matter—and to Max the restaurant represented the beginning of a shared trust, even friendship, between transgenic and ordinary.

It had been necessary, of course, to open their arts-and-crafts mall outside the boundaries of Terminal City—the toxic industrial area where they had squatted was inhabitable only by the genetically altered transgenics themselves. That Terminal City loomed across the way—a vast steel and concrete ghost town haunted by transgenic specters, a shadow of capitalism run amok, free enterprise at its worst—provided yet another irony, a sweet one, as the counterculture mall flourished, a blossoming of free enterprise at its best.

The nearby presence of Terminal City also provided an air of mystery and celebrity that attracted ordinaries to the "exotic" mall. Sketchy had hyped the mall

in the *New World Weekly*, and the rest of the media
had quickly latched on.

Max liked the fact that the transgenics now owned
the building—Logan Cale had loaned them the
money, and was well on the way to getting paid
back—and that first-floor restaurant had been re-
opened. Gem—the X5 who gave birth during the Jam
Pony crisis that ignited the Terminal City siege—
worked behind the counter, and two other X5s shared
management responsibility (where food service was
concerned, it was thought best to keep the more radi-
cally mutated transgenics behind the scenes). Most of
the Jam Pony messengers stopped there to eat when
they were making deliveries in this sector of the city,
and with the cops still on duty around the perimeter,
there was a constant threat to the doughnut inventory.

The rest of the building had been turned into the
shops of an eclectic arts and antiques mall. Those
transgenics who didn't participate artistically worked
the antiques booths. With tutoring from the former cat
burglar Max—whose street-gang mentor Moody had
taught her well, years ago, back in L.A.—the transgenic pupils learned which artifacts were worth saving and which could be ignored, not only within the
boundaries of Terminal City, but at flea markets and
dump sites throughout the city.

Sitting in the first-floor Terminal City Artworks
restaurant, nursing her cup of coffee, Max let slip a
tiny smile as she considered how much they had accomplished in so short a time.

"You look like the cat that ate the canary," Logan
Cale said as he walked up to her.

"You know I'm a vegetarian," she said.

Logan swung into the booth across from Max. "I know you're *trying* to be a vegetarian . . . How's it working out?"

She smirked. "Let's just say, next time you're ready to cook up a batch of that beefy chili of yours . . . I'm there."

Tall, with spiky dark blond hair, wire-frame glasses, and bright blue eyes, Logan Cale looked athletically fit. And, in a way, he was—maintaining a rigorous workout schedule in his modern apartment in a seemingly abandoned building just outside Terminal City's toxic borders.

But beneath his casually stylish, baggy earth-tone trousers, Logan wore an exoskeleton that gave him the ability to walk, a skill stolen from him by the bullet lodged near his spine and regained through the use of the mechanical marvel that he wore all the time now.

Though wealthy, Logan was far from being one of the idle rich. Instead, he used his money to try to fight government and private sector wrongdoing, working in support of the disadvantaged. Thus, he spent nearly every waking moment as the underground cyberjournalist that the city—and now much of the nation—knew as a mysterious voice and an image limited to those piercing blue eyes: Eyes Only. Barely a handful of people knew that Logan led this double life; another handful thought he was an agent of Eyes Only. But Max knew the truth—she had been working with him for several years now.

"I see you're reading Sketchy's latest attempt at a Pulitzer," Logan said.

"Oh yeah. He's gonna pay."

"Ooooh . . . you sound so sultry . . . enigmatic, even . . ."

She slapped at him with the tabloid, but she couldn't hold back the grin. "Coal in your stocking this year—definitely coal."

"We can always use the fuel," he said. "You know what I want for Christmas? What I really want?"

"No. But I bet you're gonna tell me."

He reached his gloved hand out and took her black leather-gloved hand in his. He squeezed. "That's what I want," he said. "Only . . . I wish it was you and me . . ."

"With the gloves off?"

He grinned, almost shyly; but what he said was rather bold: "At least."

Max loved this man.

She loved him, he loved her, and they should have been holding hands right now, really holding hands . . . Hell, they should have been living happily ever after, starting a long time ago . . .

"We should be living happily ever after, about now," she blurted, sharing the thought. "Don't you think?"

"We could be facing a much bleaker Christmas."

"Only here we sit," she said, ignoring his remark, "governing a biotech wasteland turned Jamestown for transgenics."

"Don't be so hard on the place. Or yourself. You've accomplished so much."

Calling Terminal City a Jamestown had been harsh, she knew—"Jamestown" referred to the modern-day Hoovervilles that had sprung up post-Pulse and were named after then-President Michael James. Terminal City had become much more than that.

"Yes, we could be facing a much bleaker Christmas," she finally admitted. "I don't know what's wrong with me, Logan—it's like I have an itch I can't scratch."

He gave her a look. "I know the feeling."

Max damn near blushed.

She waved for Gem to bring a cup of coffee for Logan.

The real reason she and Logan weren't living happily ever after, of course, was because of a late and very unlamented blonde bitch Max had known only as Renfro. This was back at Manticore HQ—not long before Max had burned the place to the ground— where Renfro planted a designer virus inside Max, a time bomb ticking down to kill Logan.

Basically, Renfro had made Logan allergic to Max's touch—fatally so.

Christmas always brought thoughts of home, didn't it? Max reflected. And like it or not, to her and the other transgenics—whether the "normal"-looking X5s or the mutated freaks like Joshua and Dix— Manticore had been home.

The result of genetic experimentation on a scale unheard of in the rest of the world, the Manticore refugees were freaks, and a large segment of the city still wouldn't let them forget that. After Colonel Donald Lydecker, the surrogate "father" of Manticore, had left,

Renfro assumed command. She'd been in charge when Max was captured.

Before Max's escape, Renfro and her team of conscienceless scientists—the Nazis might have relished having these "mad doctors" on staff—had injected Max with the virus, which was harmful to only one person on earth: Logan Cale. If Max and Logan touched in any way, he would get the virus . . . or rather, the virus would get him: Logan would die within twenty-four hours.

For this reason, the two were careful not to touch, and both constantly wore gloves, and long pants in the warmest of weather . . . and even in intimate situations like this one, as they sat in the restaurant in a booth, the couple kept a respectful distance, like a middle-school boy and girl on a first date.

Earlier this year they got a firsthand look at what the virus could do if it went unchecked. During Max's capture of Kelpy—the chameleon-boy-turned-serial-killer—he had somehow caught the bug. Due to Kelpy's fixation on Max, his ultimate target had been Logan, his prime goal to "become" Logan and thereby win Max's affections. When Kelpy started his chameleonlike morphing, turning him into a pseudo-Logan, Max had touched the changeling transgenic, and somehow that had been enough for the virus to be passed on—that is, to be unleashed on Kelpy.

Max and her friends—Logan, best buddy Original Cindy, Alec, Joshua, and several others—had witnessed young Kelpy's meltdown and horrifying death. Since then, Max had worked even harder to make sure that she and the man she loved never touched. Anything—the brush of a kiss, the holding of bare hands, even the most perfunctory of hugs—would be the touch of death to him.

Gem brought his coffee, placed the steaming cup in front of him and offered a warm smile, which Logan returned.

"How's Eve?" he asked the waitress.

The night after the Jam Pony hostage crisis, Gem decided that since her baby was the first transgenic to be born in freedom, the child should be named after the first woman in the world . . . hence, Eve.

"She's already standing and she wants to walk," the slim, attractive waitress said, "though she's not quite ready yet. She's gonna be a handful."

"Standing already?" Logan asked, astounded. "At six months?"

Max just smiled. "Good genes—that is, really, *really* good genes. All of us X5s did that."

Logan shook his head in wonder, then sipped his coffee as Gem returned behind the counter. Max ran a hand over her face and let out a long sigh.

"You look beat," he said. "Too bad you weren't genetically enhanced to be a mayor, not a killer."

She gave him a weak grin. "That's how tired I am—even a weak-ass crack like that made me smile."

He snorted. "Weak-ass, maybe. But you did smile."

"I did smile," Max admitted.

"And we do have much to be thankful for."

"Yes, we do. Do I sound ungrateful . . . ?"

"Oh yeah."

Max just shook her head. "Sorry . . . I wasn't wired up to be a leader . . . I'm a loner. A commando."

After taking another pull from his coffee, Logan said, "Well, loner or not, there's a whole lotta people up on the roof, asking for ya."

"Yeah?"

"Joshua, Alec, Original Cindy, Mole. I think Dix and Luke are up there. Sketchy, too . . . case you wanna toss his ass off the building."

"Now you are tempting me . . . But it's cold up there."

For most of the last two weeks, the weather had been miserable, even by Seattle's standards. The temperature had hung near the freezing mark, and the wind howling at thirty to forty miles per hour, with gusts as high as fifty.

Logan gave her a look. "I don't see you wearing a coat . . . Anyway, aren't you the one told me 'bout holding your breath for five minutes? In a pond under a sheet of ice? Back when you escaped from Manticore?"

"That doesn't mean I liked it."

"Where's your Christmas spirit?"

"Christmas at Manticore didn't build a whole lotta holiday nostalgia into me."

"How about your foster family?"

"Yeah, that was great—like when my foster father got roaring drunk and pushed my foster sister into the tree."

Shaking his head, Logan asked, "Talk about gettin' coal in your stocking, Miss Grinch. You gotta get in the Yuletide swing."

"I know a way, and it's not up on a cold rooftop."

"What's that?"

"Sitting by a fire with you. What's that old song? 'Chestnuts Roasting'?"

"See," he said, and his smile lighted up the place. "You do have some Christmas spirit in ya."

That smile of his—all those white teeth, those deep dimples. She loved his smile; she loved most everything about him. She just had a hard time saying so, and she knew he had a similar problem. But they both knew how they felt, and maybe that was enough.

The two of them had also been so busy of late that they barely saw each other. Logan continued to use Eyes Only as a positive propaganda machine for the transgenics, and Max always had some Terminal City crisis or other that needed attending. If it wasn't trouble with the water supply, it was building code violations, or choosing a logo for the new arts and antiques mall.

She might not have been interested in such mundane matters a few months ago, but now they were the tedious minutia that seemed to occupy her every waking moment. Having even a few minutes alone with Logan felt like finally coming to shore after swimming across Puget Sound.

"Why don't we just go up there," Logan suggested, "see what it is the gang wants, and be done with it?"

She playfully shook her head. "I have a better idea."

"Which is?"

"Ditch them."

His headshake was more serious. "You know we can't."

She huffed. "All right, we'll go up on the roof, we'll deal with whatever they want . . . on one condition."

"Yeah?"

"The rest of the evening—it's just us. A quiet evening together. Starting with, I'll cook you dinner. I'm gonna officially fall off the vegetarian wagon tonight."

Now, she had his attention. "Just the two of us?" he said.

"Do I stutter? Just the two of us."

She was already out of the booth, finishing her coffee on her feet, and fishing a crumpled bill out of her pocket. "Let's go."

Dix had the building's elevators running again; in fact, the mall was getting to be in such good shape, it was in danger of losing its funky appeal. Max and Logan went to the seventh floor, which was still in the process of remodeling and not yet open to the public.

At the end of the hall, the couple entered the stairway to the roof. As they climbed, they both pulled on stocking caps; they were already wearing gloves. When she started to open the door, Max felt the wind—it had sharp teeth!—try to drag the door from her grasp, and only her special strength allowed her to keep the thing from flying open all the way. Once Logan was through, she managed to push the thing closed; then she turned to see the others waiting for them under a gray sky, dusk settling on the city like a low-slung cloud.

Across the way, atop the main building of Terminal City, the Freak Nation flag flew, as straight out as a salute, stiff in the wind, its red, white, and black bars easily visible even from this distance, the rising red dove seeming to take flight.

The group standing before her in a loose semicircle, and Logan to her right, now made up her family. She smiled at the thought, feeling guilty at her reluctance to accept their invitation, flushed with warmth, despite the bitter cold, as she looked at them.

A girl could do a lot worse.

Original Cindy stood in the center, her puffball Afro mashed beneath a stocking cap pulled down over her ears, her hands conspicuous by their absence as they hid behind her back. Though an "ordinary," she was a true beauty, with lively brown eyes and a wide grin that challenged the cold.

Not one to ever be considered "ordinary" on any level, though, Original Cindy's powers were somewhat more discreet than those of Max, her best friend and sistah, her "Boo"; but Cindy's attitude was in no way discreet. Original Cindy came on like a four-hundred-pound tiger on its fifth espresso, and she didn't give a diddly damn whether anyone liked that approach or not.

Which, Max knew, was probably why O.C. and her had hit it off from the beginning, each recognizing the rebel in the other and relishing it.

On Original Cindy's right stood Alec, his dark blond hair grown out some; normally he combed those locks back, though now the wind tossed them back and forth. He had sharp dark eyes and his face bore its usual wiseass smirk; he could be a self-centered jerk, Max knew, but he had his good side.

An X5, like Max, Alec had never met a hurdle too

low to try to find a skirting shortcut; he would happily spend an hour looking for a way around a problem that he could've solved with hard work in half that time. Lately, though, Max had noticed that Alec—to his credit—had finally started to realize that what he'd once considered a gift might really be a flaw.

Next to Alec stood Joshua, the towering dog boy, the first of the Manticore experiments and now every bit a man, at least physically. His cruelly sheltered upbringing—literally in the basement of Manticore—had crippled his development, and on first meeting, you could take him for mentally challenged. Truth was, he was keenly intelligent, and had the best heart of them all. His long mane of brown hair thrashed furiously in the wind, but he seemed not to notice, his leonine face wearing a beatific smile that beamed like a lighthouse as he saw Max.

Beyond Joshua was Sketchy, the surfer bum/messenger turned tabloid journalist, another of Max's "ordinary" friends from Jam Pony. Of course, Sketchy wasn't ordinary in any sense other than that he wasn't a transgenic—tall and lanky, with stringy brown hair highlighted blond, Sketch seemed to be all knees, elbows, and bobbing head, a marionette operated by a clumsy puppeteer. The guy could be a beat behind, and often seemed to just be getting the joke the rest of the group had already finished laughing at.

To Original Cindy's left stood the two bald, albino engineers turned welding sculptors—Dix and Luke—and beyond them, the lizard man inexplicably dubbed Mole. Even in the heavy wind, Mole still chomped on an ever-present cigar.

"What's the dealio?" Max asked, practically yelling to be heard over the near gale.

The semicircle parted to reveal a large Christmas tree lashed to the corner of the roof with steel cables; the spruce—both tall and full—was strung with unlit lights and tinsel roping. Even with its heavy-duty moorings, it seemed the tree might fly off the building at any moment.

Max looked from the tree to Original Cindy, who still had her hands behind her back.

Eyes wide, Max shouted, "This had to be today?"

Original Cindy's grin faded and the rest of the group all developed a quick interest in studying their shoes.

Immediately realizing her insensitivity, Max plastered on a grin and said, "Don't get me wrong, guys—the tree rocks!"

Eyes rose to her, bright; smiles blossomed, glowing.

"It's just . . . it's so windy! It looks like any second it'll give Santa's sleigh a run for the money . . ."

Shrugging, Original Cindy said, "Weather report called for conditions to get better, later tonight, so we took a chance. Tree was gonna die if I let Normal take care of it one more day."

Reagan Ronald, aka Normal, was the manager of the Jam Pony messenger service where Max and Original Cindy had both gotten jobs when they first hit Seattle. O.C. still worked there, as did Sketchy— his journalist gig wasn't yet full-time—though Max herself hadn't been back since the hostage crisis that led to the siege at Terminal City.

During Max's tenure at Jam Pony, Normal had been a pain in the ass, with a stick up his own. The biggest thrill of his life had been receiving a signed picture of President Bush (one of 'em—Max didn't know which, not that it mattered) back in his community college days when he'd been president of the campus Young Republican club.

Max gestured to the struggling pine. "You let *Normal* take care of this tree?"

Original Cindy's smile returned. "Thas a fact."

"Our Normal? Straight-arrow, top-buttoned, stone-cold Normal?"

"I'm tellin' you, Boo, ever since he midwifed little Eve, he's one soulful white boy. Hell, he even watered the tree."

"Please tell me that didn't involve a zipper." Shaking her head, Max looked back at the tall plump tree, which still appeared to be struggling against the cables. "That must have taken up damn near alla Jam Pony!"

"Purt near . . . hey, but we roll with it, right?"

"I can't believe Normal went along with this."

"You wanna really lose your mind?" O.C. looked around conspiratorially. "It was Normal's *brainstorm*."

"Normal's idea."

"Gettin' you guys this tree, swear on my mama, Boo."

"Well, where is he, then?"

"Hey! Cut the man some slack, my sistah—gotta at least let 'im *pretend* he's still an asshole."

Max was gazing at the tree; feelings of warmth were stirring in her, out on this frigid rooftop. "Well, God bless Normal . . . 'cause this is beautiful."

Taking a hand out from behind her back, Original Cindy offered Max a black metal cube with a silver toggle switch. "Dix and Luke—their latest black box . . . Honor's yours, Boo."

Lump in her throat, Max took the box, and glanced at her two egghead, eggheaded friends, who both nodded vigorously; then she flipped the switch. Colored lights came on all over the tree, red and white and green and blue, twinkling, sparkling, shimmering, the star at the top shining bright white, colored balls bobbling, a glowing vision in the twilight.

"It's beautiful," Max said again, her voice hushed.

She turned to the man at her side; Logan smiled at her. The rest of the group gathered round, each taking a turn hugging Max. Even Alec—who rarely touched anyone, other than the occasional one-night-stand female he deigned with his passing presence—gave in.

All but Logan.

He stayed a step or two back—as usual, she and he were aware of the required distance between them.

"This is gonna be a dope spot for watchin' the comet, Christmas Eve," Original Cindy pointed out.

The whole country was awaiting the arrival of the so-called Christmas star, the once-every-two-thousand-years passing of a comet that some astronomers thought might also have been the fabled star of Bethlehem.

Max smirked. "According to Sketchy's rag, the comet signals the end of the world."

"According to Sketchy's rag," Original Cindy said, "Elvis is coming back New Year's, on a flyin' saucer."

The group gathered closer to the edge of the

rooftop, getting a good look at the glowing, colorful tree. Max studied every light, every colored ball. The tree was magnificent. She had always considered Christmas a corny relic of pre-Pulse decadence. But now she understood what the fuss was about . . . family, friends . . . and she could think of no better present than this. The tree would be visible for miles around, and people far away from Terminal City would still be able to see the Freaks' Christmas tree on top of their new mall.

They had indeed come a long way in a short time.

She was still contemplating this when, moments later, the wind expressed its own, less sentimental opinion, grabbing the tree and shaking it even more violently than it had up till now, like an abusive parent manhandling a naughty child.

Logan reflexively reached for the tree, to haul it back, but the wind shifted again, this time coming across and sweeping the tree back upright and to the left, the branches slapping Logan, sweeping him off balance. His eyes went wide, white all around, as he teetered for a moment—his balance good in the exoskeleton, but not perfect, he wasn't as nimble as he'd been—and, in proof of that reality, he pitched back over the edge without a sound.

Max had seen it coming but had no time to warn him, much less reach him in time. All she could do was throw herself toward the roof's edge, her hand extending out in front of her and over the side. At the last possible instant, she caught Logan's gloved hand in hers, and then he dangled seven stories over the city, a human Christmas ornament.

Max's arm threatened to tear itself from its socket, in this effort to defeat gravity and keep Logan from falling. Alec and Joshua, moving quickly, each grabbed one of her legs and started pulling her away from the edge and thus raising Logan. Original Cindy and Mole had hopped to either side of Max, their hands extended down over the side, too, waiting for the first chance to get their hands on Logan and wrestle him back onto the roof.

Max concentrated on holding onto the man she loved, just keeping him alive and letting the others do the work. As long as it was only their gloves touching, everything would be all right. Logan swung closer now, and Mole and O.C. each grabbed a shoulder and started tugging. Mole got a good hold and jerked, and suddenly Max saw Logan coming back up over the edge . . . his head flying right toward the flesh of her uncovered face!

Lurching backward, Max jerked her head out of the way as Logan crashed down on top of her.

They were touching everywhere, but Max wasn't terribly concerned about that—they were bundled up, and other than their faces, their skin was not exposed. They both moved carefully as they untangled.

Max could see Original Cindy and the others shouting, but she was concentrating so hard on not touching Logan that she didn't hear a word anyone was saying now. Just as they slid apart, a gust of wind came up from behind her. She braced her body, but there was nothing to be done as the gale swept her hair up and into Logan's face, her stocking hat flying off and over the side.

She could feel the electrical charge exchanged between her hair and his face, as her corrupted DNA met his vulnerable DNA. He gasped, and in that second of contact, Max died inside, knowing that those wisps of her hair had just sentenced the man she loved to death.

Everybody froze.

Her eyes locked with Logan's, and his look said that he knew the truth as well as she did.

In less than twenty-four hours, he would be dead. They both knew the drill by now: they had been through it before. On two previous occasions, the symptoms had erupted and nearly done him in. Both times a miracle had saved him, but this time they knew no miracle would be in the offing. No one had discovered the cure, and the only vial of antigen that existed had long since been used up.

Logan found his voice first. "I'm . . . I'm sorry."

That almost made her break down.

She'd just killed him, and *he* was apologizing?

Max knew, hearing those two pitiful words, that she couldn't get through this. There was no way she could watch Logan go down this horrible road again. First there would be the fever, then the chills, the sweats, the seizures, and from there on a rapid downhill slide to the bottom of the abyss . . .

But after only a moment's consideration, she also knew there was nowhere else for her to go. If Logan was going to die, she would be at his side until the end . . .

. . . even if it killed her, too.

Chapter Three
DEATH WATCH

That Logan's apartment seemed warm and cozy, made a bitter parody of the evening Max had envisioned for them earlier.

After making their way through the underground passageway leading from Terminal City to the clandestine apartment, Logan—surprisingly, not showing any signs of the virus kicking in, as yet—had called his old friend Dr. Sam Carr, neurosurgeon at Metro Medical Hospital and Logan's personal physician. Carr was part of that small handful of confidants who knew that Logan and Eyes Only were one and the same.

Then the couple had settled in to wait. They were together atop Logan's bed, lying there in each other's arms. At first she kept the usual respectful distance, on the longshot chance that by some fluke the brushing of her hair against his flesh had not been enough to jumpstart the virus. . . .

But Logan said, "No point in us not touching anymore, is there?"

And he enfolded her in an embrace, so that now she lay in his arms, in their warmth, a warmth matching the apartment, the bedroom itself. She was reminded, strangely, of the night she and the others, her siblings, had escaped from Manticore.

How odd—that icy night in Gillette, Wyoming, seemed so far from this time, this place. Only the kindness of a stranger—the Manticore nurse Hannah, who'd taken the frightened X5 into the inviting hospitality of her heated cabin—had prevented the young girl from freezing to death before she'd got a taste of real freedom. That tiny one-room cabin in the middle of nowhere had provided the nine-year-old with her first glimpse of a life, a home, that could be more than just an antiseptic dormitory.

In many ways, Max had been on a search to recapture that feeling of warmth every day since—she'd experienced that warmth in Logan's presence, periodically. Now, with him really next to her, holding her, she finally had that feeling again, in so complete—and yet terrible—a way. A tear trickled down her cheek, and he wiped it away, almost absently.

By comparison to that cabin, this apartment—contrived out of a vacant, Cale-family-owned building just outside the borders of Terminal City—was a palace. The bed alone seemed nearly as big as the one-room cabin back in Wyoming. The rest of the room's furnishings reflected a spare masculinity typical of Logan—dresser, armoire, and two nightstands. There was a four-door closet that took up much of the far wall. Logan's laptop atop the dresser was turned on, its screensaver of Earth, as seen from the surface of the moon, providing the only major light source.

Next to the dresser, a small stereo unit quietly played classical music. Max didn't know the piece and wasn't consciously listening, really; but the strings seemed to soothe something within her. If she could just get that feeling to last for more than thirty seconds at a time . . .

She drew away slightly, leaned on an elbow and studied him—he looked fine. Normal, even. She hated to ask, but she had to: "How do you feel?"

He shrugged. "I have to say . . . okay, really. Shaken, but mostly by the . . . thought of what's coming."

"But it came on faster than this before," she said.

They had only been in the bedroom a few minutes, but it had taken at least five to reach the apartment and a minute or two on the phone, reaching Carr; the couple was alone in the apartment, the rest of the group allowing them their privacy as the death watch got under way. Maybe as much as ten minutes had passed since her DNA and his had commingled . . .

The other times the designer virus had reared its ugly head, the onset of symptoms had been almost instantaneous. This lull before the shit storm confused them both.

Logan was propped on an elbow, too, looking right at her. "Maybe . . . I've worked up some immunity? From having it before. Might take longer to present."

She shook her head. "I don't think so. Didn't happen that way the last time."

Logan's eyes widened and he shrugged again. "It's weird as hell, Max . . . but I feel all right. I feel good."

"How long has it been?"

"Since we first touched?"

She nodded.

He checked his wristwatch. "Almost fifteen minutes."

A tempest roiled in Max's belly, and not even the strings in the classical music could soothe her now. The fear and despair were mixing it up with hope— who was it that said, "It's not the despair, I can handle the despair . . . it's the hope!"

Nonetheless, something *was* different this time. Logan should have been sweating profusely by now, in the merciless grip of chills, with seizures not far 'round the corner. Yet he felt warm against her—not feverish. He smelled good, that fresh cocktail of aftershave and powder she knew so well—as if he'd spruced up for her, anticipating that this evening might be the night of love they'd both longed for, a honeymoon about to happen, not a damn death watch. She loved the aroma and took it deep into her lungs, feeling greedy for it, knowing this sensation was one that would likely have to last her the rest of her life.

She heard a faint knock. Logan didn't react, but she sat up, just as the knock repeated, this time more forcefully, and Logan jumped a little next to her.

"Gotta love a doctor who makes house calls," he said as he started to sit up.

Max pushed him back down into the pillow and climbed off the bed herself. "You stay right here, mister—you're the patient, I'm the nurse, and I'll fetch the doctor. Chain of command, clear?"

"Yes, ma'am."

But she was already out of the bedroom and into the large room with its dividers that cordoned-off sections. The kitchen, with all its postmodern stainless steel appliances, and the dining area, with an oak table large enough for six, were off to her right. The apartment was similar to the one Ames White and his NSA minions had trashed last year, with a comforting familiarity about it—like the living room with its monstrous leather sofa, three chairs, coffee table, and lawn-sized area rug, directly in front of her, and Logan's office space to her left in the rear of the spacious quarters. A door at the far end of the room led to the tunnel that connected them to Terminal City, and the door to the right, the one that Dr. Sam Carr was presumably pounding on now, opened to the street.

After a quick check of the small monitor to one side of the entry—a video peephole of sorts—Max flung the door open to reveal Dr. Carr in a heavy blue parka, the hood pulled up to protect the man's balding head from the wind. A gust whipped into the apartment, helping Carr inside. He and Max didn't even bother to speak until the door was firmly bolted against the nasty weather.

"Where is he?" Carr asked, handing Max his Gladstone bag, then slipping off his coat and hanging it over the back of a dinner-table chair.

Perhaps five-ten, with a forehead that stopped at the

apex of his skull, Carr had short dark hair that covered the back and sides of his oval-shaped head like a
yarmulke with flaps. His dark eyes had the resigned
sadness tinged with kindness of a man who'd spent a
career listening to people's problems; his nose was
long and straight, his mouth sensitive, his chin cleft.

"Bedroom," Max said.

"How'd it happen? You've been careful."

She told him.

"Be surprised how many people die stupidly
around Christmas." Shaking his head, Carr took the
Gladstone bag from her. "Frankly, I don't know what
I can do for him. We can try a transfusion from another transgenic, but—"

"Don't you usually examine a patient first, then
make your diagnosis and treatment?"

Carr's eyes tensed. "What's going on here, Max?"

"That's what I'd like to know—go look him over."

She was trying to keep the hope out of her voice,
and Carr seemed to be reading that as despair, keeping his eyes on her even as he crossed to the bedroom,
where he slipped inside.

Max flopped onto the couch, trying to force all
feeling and emotion from herself. Let the doctor
do his work—let him examine his patient, and science would determine whether Logan Cale had a
future . . .

She didn't dare embrace these hopeful feelings. It
was going on half an hour since her hair blew into
Logan's face, and he seemed fine. But how could that
be so? Renfro herself—Manticore's final leader—had

told Max there was no cure, and no antidote but for that small vial of antigen, which was long gone.

The detestable woman had proceeded to take a bullet for Max, saving the X5 for some unknown reason, then dying in her captive's arms, saving Max from death . . . but leaving the young woman cursed with that designer virus . . .

In a way, hope had been the bane of Max's existence, and—like a prisoner with a life sentence—she had tried to avoid that particular emotion; but, like a nagging summer cold, it just kept coming back. She knew that her probably naive wellspring of hope was how she differed from Zack, her brother and the leader of the twelve who escaped Manticore, or impulsive Seth who'd not made it out that first night, and from Brin, who was reindoctrinated by Renfro, even from self-centered Alec, who had shown signs of coming around some lately, but who was still, at his core, a cynic.

Among the X5s, only Jondy and Tinga seemed to carry hope inside them in the way Max did, and one of them—Jondy—had disappeared, while the other, Tinga, was dead. And yet Joshua, the first of the experiments, despite all he'd suffered, had never lost hope; locked up in the basement of Manticore—an unwanted stepchild following the disappearance of that benign father known only as Sandeman—Joshua had nothing *but* hope.

It was an argument for certain qualities, positive or negative, being born into a person—she'd always said Joshua had a good heart, and where hope in Max was a flicker compared to her inner fire of rage, in Joshua hope radiated, and all the cruelty leveled upon him could never snuff that flame.

Maybe Joshua had been right to hope in the face of despair—still, to Max, hope seemed to bring nothing but disappointment . . . which did not prevent her from hoping with all her heart that Sam Carr could do something to save Logan.

When the doctor had been in with Logan for over an hour, Max was starting to fear the worst. She longed to break down the closed door and find out what was going on, but she forced herself to stay in the living room, pretending to read an art book of Logan's.

Finally, unable to take it anymore, she tossed the book on the sofa and got to her feet. Pacing now, she felt slightly better—any activity was better than none. She marched over to the door, listened intently, her rabbit's ears picking up nothing but what sounded like mumbling, then she stalked to the other end of the room.

Stopping at the door that led to the tunnel, she had the sudden urge to simply bolt. Running away, leaving the pain behind, knowing she would never connect with another person as she had with Logan . . . wouldn't that be better than staying here to suffer this loss?

But it was only a moment—only a fleeting thought. As much as the urge to flee might gnaw at her, the need to stay overrode it. She turned and trudged back toward the bedroom.

Max was only a few steps away when the door opened and Logan came out, Carr trailing him.

And Logan looked fine. In fact, he looked wonderful—he was wearing a wide smile and holding open his arms to her. Her eyes shot to Carr, who shrugged and smiled too, though the doctor's smile was lopsided, digging a groove of uncertainty in one cheek.

"What are you two grinning about?" she asked, almost irritated. She did not step into Logan's offered embrace.

Carr came forward, holding up a small black box that looked like a voltage meter. "Blood test showed no sign of the virus."

Max's eyes traveled from Carr to Logan and back to Carr; she pushed the hope down—it was leaping within her like an eager puppy, and she would not acknowledge it. "How in hell can *that* be?"

Logan finally realized that Max wasn't going to fall into his arms, and dropped his hands to his sides; but his smile didn't fade.

"That's what took so long," he said. "We've been doing some impromptu research on the laptop, trying to make sense of it."

"And did you?"

The doctor said, "I know it's a lot to take in—I won't lie to you and say I've taken it all in, sufficiently, myself." He motioned to the couch. "Let's sit down and take this a step at a time . . . and I'll do my best to explain the theory we've come up with."

They moved into the living room area, Max still doubtful, and a little shellshocked, as she took a seat on the leather couch. Logan sat next to her, very close, and she fought the urge to scoot away from him—maintaining distance was a habit now.

Carr took a seat in one of the chairs facing them. "As I said, I did the blood test and there's no sign of the virus."

She looked from Carr to Logan, whose own grin had turned lopsided, too—he seemed almost embarrassed, for some reason.

"Do we need to take Logan to a facility," she asked, "and check again?"

The doctor's eyebrows lifted. "You mean, do we need a second opinion? We asked ourselves that, but this is a simple procedure. We didn't need an opinion—we needed an explanation."

"So you went to the laptop. And?"

Logan jumped in. "Actually, first we discussed it a while—we couldn't just do this randomly. We had to start with a theory, or theories, and work from there. The only thing I could come up with involves Kelpy."

She frowned. "What could *he* have to do with it? All Kelpy proved is how virulent this thing is! We saw how quickly, how . . . horribly, he—"

Logan silenced her with a raised palm. "Think for a moment, Max—the only significant event relating to the virus, in all these months, has been Kelpy's contact with me, and with you. His death, when he 'became' me, and died accordingly, is the only change in circumstance."

She mulled that. "We had been careful, for a long, long time."

"Yes," Logan said. "You and I have been extremely careful since my last exposure."

"Until tonight, anyway."

"And what happened tonight?"

"We touched—my hair blew in your face, and . . ."

"And what?"

"And . . . nothing, so far."

"Yes. And I began to ask myself—had Kelpy some-how died in my place? When he took on my physi-cality, he obviously became subject to the virus . . . otherwise, he wouldn't have died."

Nodding, she said, "You passed that capacity to Kelpy, Logan—but *I* passed the virus to him!"

"Yes. Now stay with me . . . I hacked into Manticore records and learned more about Kelpy. Seems when he 'blended,' some of the changes took place on a genetic level, as well."

Again Max frowned in thought. "A kind of bio-chemical morphing?"

Carr picked up the thread. "In a manner of speak-ing," the doctor said. "It wasn't true morphing—he stopped short of that, most of the changes physiolog-ical but not genetic. He essentially assumed the shell of whoever he was trying to blend in with."

"All of which means what?" Max asked.

Logan said, "That enough of his changes *were* ge-netic to fool the virus."

Slowly, as if repeating a child's ridiculous assertion, Max said, "Fool . . . the . . . virus?"

"Yeah. The virus thought Kelpy was me."

"The virus . . . *thought* . . . ?"

Carr said, "That's just a convenient way of express-ing the concept that this virus was 'programmed' to kill Logan. It recognized Kelpy as Logan and that's why the virus attacked him. When its target was dead, it became inert."

"Is that even possible?"

"Very much so," Carr said with an assertive nod. "The scientists at Manticore were operating on the highest levels of genetic engineering . . . but I guess I don't have to tell you that."

"No," Max said dryly.

"The irony is, two of their creations—one of which was designed to take you down, Max—collided, and inadvertently destroyed each other . . . and saved you and Logan from what we now know would have been an inevitable tragedy."

"Even with all our precautions," Logan said, "we were kidding each other that we'd never touch . . . but we couldn't stay apart, could we?"

She just looked at him.

Logan reached out to put his arm around her. She jumped up, away from him.

"This is whack," she said. "Doctor, tell him not to touch me—we can't be sure, we can't know . . ."

Carr said, "Logan, she's right. We need—"

But Logan was on his feet, clearly irritated. "Damnit, Max—sometimes the news is *good* . . . It's over. That goddamned virus is out of our lives."

Max looked past Logan at Carr. She felt irritated, too—though she knew she should be happy. Wasn't this the news they had been waiting over a year to hear?

"Dr. Carr," she said evenly, "I want to believe it, but I can't. I'm afraid that this thing will come back, that this . . . this remission is just a fluke. You said I was right to be careful. What do we need to do to make sure?"

Logan, frustrated, turned to Carr and said, "You agree, Sam, that—"

Carr patted the air. "Logan, Max is skeptical and she's cautious—traits that have served her well." Now the doctor spoke to Max: "We'll do a blood test on you, and *then* we'll have an answer."

"A definitive answer?" she asked.

Logan was shaking his head. "My God, Max—you can see the dark cloud in every silver lining."

"Very little is definitive in this world, Max," the doctor said. "Particularly in this post-Pulse world . . . Now, if the virus is still inside you, it might be inert or it might merely be dormant."

Hands on hips, she asked, "And your little black blood-test box can tell us?"

"Yes."

She shrugged. "Then let's do it."

"Bedroom," Carr said, gesturing.

Moments later, Logan and Max sat on the bed, somewhat apart, as Carr went to work. First, he swabbed her arm with alcohol, then with a needle removed a few CCs of blood. He gave her another swab to press against the wound.

"Take just a minute," he said reassuringly.

He inserted the needle into a rubberized receptacle in his black box and pumped in the blood. Carr's fingers expertly touched various buttons on the front of the box, and then paused, as if he'd dialed a cell phone and was waiting for a response. Carr studied the box's small LCD screen, then he pushed another button.

"I'm printing a readout," the doctor said. "I know you like things in black and white, Max . . ."

A moment later a slip of paper, like a gas station receipt, came rolling out the bottom of the box. Carr tore it off and handed it to Max. Down the left side were abbreviations, down the right side numbers. She read the list but it meant nothing to her. She held it up, her eyebrows rising in question.

"See any zeroes?" Carr asked.

She looked at the list again. "Yeah. Fourth one down."

"What's it say in the left column?"

"V.I."

"Viruses," Carr said. "V.I. stands for viruses . . . and you're reading zero. You don't even have a mild flu bug, Max."

"I'm . . . clean."

"The virus is out of your system."

Max just sat there—she felt numb. It was as if Carr were suddenly three rooms away. "No virus?"

"Apparently Kelpy absorbed it out of your system. It's possible his capacity to blend, to morph, went slightly haywire when, in his Logan phase, you and he touched and instinctively he began to take on some of your characteristics—suddenly the human chameleon was the carrier *and* the recipient."

Logan said, "So, then . . . the virus killed Kelpy . . . and itself."

Carr sighed, shrugged. "Without both of you entering into a lengthy research program at some top facility," the doctor said, "we will likely never know for sure."

Logan smiled. "Maybe it was magic."

She turned to Logan, and he was grinning like an

idiot; then she looked at Carr, and he wore a big smile, too.

"Really . . . gone?" she asked.

Carr nodded slowly. "If I might prescribe something? Allow yourself to feel relieved . . . and happy."

Max turned to Logan, wrapped her arms around him and kissed him hard and deep and for a very long time. At first surprised, Logan got into the swing of things quickly.

Finally, Carr said, "Hey, you two—get a room!"

They broke their kiss off, and Logan said, "This *is* my room. You're the sicko voyeur, Sam."

Carr seemed about to make a potentially amusing remark, when Max bounded off the bed and grabbed the doctor by the elbow and started leading him out of the bedroom.

"Whoa, whoa," he protested. "My bag!"

Behind them, Logan picked up the bag, put the black box inside, and followed them into the main room.

Logan said, "Sam, I don't know how to thank you."

"I do," Max said.

And kissed him on the cheek.

Carr looked at her, apparently amazed that this tough little woman could be so tender.

"Thanks, Doc," she said. "You're a lifesaver—literally. It really is a shame you have to leave so soon."

Carr was chuckling as Max—maintaining a fast pace—helped him into his parka and Logan handed him the Gladstone bag. At the door, Max gave him another quick kiss on the cheek and said, "Thank you, Sam."

"You're welcome," he said.

He was only halfway through "welcome" when she shoved him outside into the night and the howling wind, and Carr managed to say, "Name it after me," before she shut the door in his face.

Twisting the dead bolt into place, Max turned to face Logan. "I thought he'd never go."

But now that she was happy, his smile had disappeared; suddenly Logan looked serious.

That was okay—what was about to happen between them *was* serious . . . the consummation of a love that had been forced into a state of limbo by that dead virus. She crossed her arms at her waist and grabbed the hem of her shirt, about to pull it over her head.

Stepping forward, he put his hands on top of hers to stop her. "We have to talk."

"That's usually the woman's line."

"I know."

"Your timing is kinda lousy, don't ya think?"

His eyes were filled with love, but also something else—sadness? "Max . . . nothing means more to me than you . . . and loving you. But there's something . . ."

She sighed. "Did I ever tell you about the tiny bit of cat DNA they slipped into me? That sends me into heat three times a year?"

He nodded.

"Well, it's about that time . . ." She raised her eyebrows. "What's wrong, Logan? We've been waiting—"

"I know, I know. But we have to be honest with each other. This isn't just animal magnetism, Max—

if we're going to be together—and I don't mean just *that* way . . . well . . ."

He took her by the hand, led her to the sofa and gestured for her to sit.

The mood had shifted, and Max was bewildered. Sitting, she asked, "What's the matter?"

He removed his glasses and rubbed a hand over his face. Then he said, "This isn't easy, Max . . . but I need to tell you something."

"You slept with Asha," she said matter-of-factly.

She meant Asha Barlow, the slim blonde S1W revolutionary Logan had teamed up with when Max had been presumed dead.

"Don't care," she said. "Old news."

This sucker-punched him. "What are you talking about?"

"You mean, you *didn't* sleep with Asha?"

"No! Hell, no."

"She's very beautiful."

"Max, please. I was . . . mourning you . . . Why would you even think that?"

She shrugged. "Sounded like you were going into confession mode . . . Just thought I'd hurry things up, so we move this along, and could get back to more important matters . . ."

But Logan, brow furrowed, was a step behind. "You thought I slept with Asha?"

"You believed I was dead, you were lonely . . ."

"I *didn't.*"

She smiled. "Cool. Even better, now . . ."

"But I do have something . . . something to confess."

She sat back, crossed her arms; there was no

turning him back now. He was going to get this out in the open, whatever the hell he was yammering about.

"Okay," she said, "spill your terrible secret. Bisexual? Don't care. All your family money's gone? So what."

His eyes met hers. "Max . . . it's about Seth."

She tensed. "Seth . . . my brother, Seth?"

"I knew him, Max."

One of the X5s who had tried to escape that night back in Wyoming, Seth had been caught by the Manticore guards. He escaped at a later date, and Max—living in Los Angeles at the time—had tracked him to Seattle. They were reunited at the top of the Space Needle in 2019, ten years after Max split from Manticore. The reunion had been short-lived: Seth died that night, plummeting from the top of the Needle.

"When we first met, Max, you'll recall I knew a lot about the X5s and Manticore . . . Not information the average guy on the street is privy to."

"What do you mean . . . you 'knew' Seth?"

"On the needle that night—those people you interrupted . . ."

"The bad guys."

"Bad guys, right—they were involved in criminal activities that Eyes Only wanted to stop."

"*You're* Eyes Only, Logan."

". . . Yes."

"You mean . . . Seth was working for you that night."

All Logan could do was nod.

"I wasn't the first X5 you recruited, then."

"No. Seth."

She felt tears welling. "That night at the Needle, taking on Jared Sterling and all those Koreans—Seth was on a mission for Eyes Only."

Logan's voice seemed small. "Yes."

"And he died. He got killed. You got him killed."

". . . I know. I've had to live with that a long time."

Something burned in her stomach and rose to the back of her throat. Swallowing hard, she got it down, but just barely. *This couldn't be happening—not now, not when the virus was vanquished and nothing stood between their love . . .*

Except betrayal.

And lies.

She rose and her eyes locked with his—his had a terrible softness, while hers blazed. "There were nearly a dozen men there that night—the Koreans, Sterling and his own thugs—and you sent Seth in there *alone*."

"I did."

She glared at him, her lips curled in anger. "And you never *told* me? Not until *now*?"

He shook his head and gave her a pathetic little shrug. "We all have our secrets, Max. You didn't tell me everything, not at first."

"You've known all there is to know about me for a long, long time. I've leveled with you; I've opened myself to you in a way I haven't to anybody, ever." Her voice was rising in pitch and intensity, but she couldn't seem to stop it. "You don't *not* tell someone something like this by . . . by accident. This was no oversight. It's willful, Logan—you *lied* to me."

He swallowed thickly. "In a way."

"For what?" She was almost shrieking now. "Why? Why would you lie to me? *Me?*"

"At first, you were . . . how can I say this?"

"Find a way."

"You were just the second recruit . . . and if I told you what had become of the first X5 I'd taken on, you might . . ."

"Hesitate to get my ass killed for you?"

Logan winced. "Something like that. And then . . . as we grew close . . . I just couldn't find a way. You made it clear how deep your love and commitment for your siblings ran . . . and for me to admit causing the death of one of them, I was afraid . . ."

"Afraid of what I'd do to you?"

"Afraid you'd hate me."

"Good call."

He stood staring at her as if she'd punched him.

Her tears ran now—hot tears of sorrow-tinged anger as she thought about Seth, and the man she loved who'd got him killed, this man in front of her, the man who was supposed to love her. "Were you *ever* going to tell me?"

"Max . . . I just did."

"Oh, so better late than never?"

Logan said nothing.

"You kept me dangling," she said, "so I'd continue to do your bidding—serve your various self-righteous agendas . . . same as you did with Seth. You couldn't tell me because you might lose a valuable resource in Eyes Only's crusade."

"It wasn't that at all."

"What the hell was it then?"

"Max . . . you know what it was."

"Do I?"

". . . I fell in love with you."

Now she felt as though he had punched her; but she lashed back, "And you figured that telling me you got my brother killed might put a damper on my feelings?"

"Max, I—"

"Don't 'Max' me—I'm maxed out. I've heard enough."

She crossed the room, snatching her jacket off the back of a dining room chair as she went.

Going the opposite way around the couch, he headed her off at the door and put a hand on her arm.

"Want that broken?" she asked, glancing down at the offending hand.

He didn't move.

"Fair warning." She grabbed his hand in hers, removed it from her arm and was about to crush it.

Logan made no effort to stop her—he just stood there staring into her eyes, the pain in his having nothing to do with the pressure she was applying.

Applying more, she saw the first flash of physical pain in his face and released her grip.

"Hell with it," she snarled. "I'm outta here."

She threw the door open and strode out into a night almost as angry as she was, leaving Logan behind with his lies and his guilt, standing in the doorway, the wind chastising him.

He called her name once, but she ignored him and stalked off into the darkness. Tonight, she wouldn't go back to Terminal City, wouldn't worry about the inhabitants. She couldn't be near any of them tonight, not even Joshua and Original Cindy. The only place to be tonight was where she had last seen her brother—where Seth had died.

The Space Needle was pretty much as she remembered it, even though she hadn't been there since the Terminal City siege began. There were a few new graffiti tags, but other than that, the Needle was same-o same-o. Turning on the power, which few but Max knew still allowed the elevators to run, she rode up to the observation deck, then climbed some more until she got out to her usual perch at the very top.

The wind whipped even worse this high, but she was careful, and her jacket was warm, and besides, from up here she could feel close to Seth and maybe gain some perspective.

Over five hundred feet below her the city went about its usual nighttime activities, signaled by fireplay flickerings across the landscape, seeming very small. Up here, so far removed from everything, she felt small, too, and tonight, somewhat insignificant.

So many years, so many failures.

And not just her failures—sometimes, like this time, the failure lay with someone else. Logan could have told me, she thought, should have told me. Hell, he'd had over two years to find a way to break this to her, and yet he had never brought it up until tonight.

The tears were streaming again. You're not so tough, she told herself. That flame of hope she'd kept within herself, that she had never allowed to flicker out—sometimes it seemed those rays of hope were all she really had that belonged to her.

Now, just as he'd gotten Seth killed, Logan had doused that tiny flame. Only despair remained, and an icy, enveloping cold.

Chapter Four

VANISHED

SEATTLE, WASHINGTON
DECEMBER 21, 2021

By the next morning the wind had subsided some, but the thirty degree temperature lingered, a guest overstaying its welcome. Come dawn, Max had finally abandoned her perch atop the Needle. As morning bled into the sky, she felt an urge to climb on her Ninja and just keep riding; she might have given in to that impulse if the bike hadn't been sitting back in Terminal City.

And right now she just didn't have the heart to go back there and face her friends, and their questions . . .

Wandering into the city as it woke, Max purchased two cups of coffee at a bakery, balancing them atop a box of bagels, and found herself walking on a kind of autopilot up to the entrance of her former place of employment—Jam Pony Express. Except where pockmarks remained from bullets fired at the building during the hostage crisis six months ago, the place hadn't really changed since the night when Max left that life behind.

The usual morning hubbub buzzed around the place, that peculiar combination of weariness and energy, of chaos and organization, found at the top of the day in most any workplace. The little ramp that led down to the concrete floor was swept neatly, as usual, and the wire grating that separated Normal—the messenger service's manager—from his peons still looked like this was visiting day at county lockup . . . though whether it was the messengers who were the prisoners, or Normal, remained unclear.

Several of Normal's seemingly endless supply of disheveled young riders milled about, sipping coffee or chatting each other up, some getting ready to take off on their first runs of the day. A few recognized Jam Pony's most famous graduate and stared openly at Max.

The peaceful settlement of the Terminal City siege had actually made her a local celebrity of sorts. Not reacting to those watching her, Max wondered if this was how Jenny Brooks, the Channel 7 weather girl, felt when she walked the streets.

This fifteen minutes of fame—which seemed to keep renewing itself—was surprisingly hard on Max, who as a loner felt uncomfortable wearing the eyes of others, and who as a longtime fugitive—she had spent most of her life on the run from Manticore, after all—felt uneasy when she could not fade into the landscape.

Doing her best to ignore the stares, she picked up on Normal, active behind his wire window. He had not changed an iota—his blondish hair was cut in its usual flat top, his black glasses continued to try to flee down his nose, and his ever-present earpiece made him look like the world's least sophisticated cyborg. He landed behind the window and looked up—sensing someone just standing there motionless, which meant a messenger needed a reprimand, of course— and then his mouth creased into something that might have been a smile.

"Well, well, little missy," he said. He always seemed to savor his words, as if each one was his favorite flavor Lifesaver. "Have you finally come crawling back looking for your job?"

She gave him a good-natured smirk. "That's right, Normal—the money we're making hand-over-fist at the Terminal City Mall just can't compare to the nickels and dimes you used to toss me."

He pretended to frown. "Well, that's a good thing— because I don't have an opening right now."

"Oh, damn. I'm crushed." She set the box of bagels on the counter and removed the two cups of coffee from their perch. She turned to find half a dozen messengers standing around her, watching their exchange. Max stopped, feeling awkward.

"Yes, slackers, it's Max—as seen on TV," Normal said pleasantly. Then he scowled and yelled: "Get moving! This is not a youth hostel, but I *am* hostile to youth—packages to be delivered, people—bip bip bip!"

Slowly, grumbling, the group broke up.

Turning back to Normal, she laughed. "That's a new one—hostel, hostile? Nice."

Around them, kids were still watching as they threaded off, and Normal's response was only to shoot Max a cross look; then when all of the messengers had moved along, none of them wanting to be next in line to feel Normal's wrath, the crew-cut petty dictator flashed her an affectionate smile.

"Truth is, missy," he said, "you always got a home here, if you want it."

She tilted her head. "You're getting soft, Normal."

"Hey, I said there was a place for you, when this celebrity stuff wears off and you need to make a living again . . . but you'll have to carry your weight."

"Actually, you didn't say there was a 'place' for me, Normal. You said 'home' . . . and Normal . . . that was nice to hear. You haven't chased off your 'Nubian princess,' have ya?"

He pointed with his chin toward the cluster of lockers at the back. "She's here all right—the granddam of Jam Pony . . ."

"That's Original Cindy, all right."

"Oh yeah—only this morning she seems sorta out of sorts . . . Maybe it's female trouble."

"Why don't you go over to her, Normal, and suggest she take somethin' for that? Then you'll find out what female trouble is all about."

Normal almost blushed. "I just mean . . . she's down. Blue. Cranky I'm used to—her in the dumps, that's somethin' else . . . Go say hello to her."

"Well, jeez, Normal . . . are you concerned for one of your people?"

"If she has a bad day, I have a bad day . . . by which I mean, my packages don't get delivered on time."

"Right."

And she grinned at him.

It was infectious, and he turned away, getting back to work, hiding his humanity.

As she strolled toward the back, Max shook her head, surprised at how nice it was to see Normal. Who'da thunk she'd have missed that stick-up-the-butt goofus? The truth was, despite a longstanding prejudice against the transgenics, when she and her fellows had really needed him, Normal came through in a big way.

A stand-up guy, with a good heart . . . amazing.

It felt surprisingly good to be here, back on her old stomping grounds, with people she could depend on, unlike a certain cyberjournalist. After moving to the back of the huge, rank room—funny, she hadn't ever noticed the sweat-drenched scent of the place before—she found her best friend sitting on a bench facing her locker, head bowed as if in prayer.

Original Cindy's Afro was flying at half mast today, brushed down and pulled back into a puff at the back of her skull. She was in jeans and a gray vintage GRRRRL POWER! sweatshirt that looked rumpled, almost slept-in—a rarity for a woman whose wardrobe was always as sharp as she was.

"Anyone for coffee?" Max asked, holding out the cardboard cup.

Original Cindy's eyes shot up to her—eyes that were red-rimmed either from crying or lack of sleep or both. Then the shapely woman was on her feet and taking her friend in her arms, damn near causing Max to dump the two cups of coffee all over everything.

"Hey hey hey," Max said, doing a balance act as Cindy hugged her. "Careful, girl—you'll spill the joe!"

"Where you been keepin' yourself, Boo?" Original Cindy demanded, backing away but not letting go of Max, her expression alternating between relief and indignation. "Damn, girl! We spent all night looking for your ass."

Shrugging, Max said, "I had some thinking to do."

"So you had some thinkin' to do—thass cool. Only you know what is *not* cool? Leavin' your brothers and sisters hangin', all crazyass-worried and shit."

"I'm sorry," Max said, and this had not occurred to her at all. "It's just . . . things went kinda sideways . . . with Logan."

"Yeah, I know, details at eleven . . . What, you think he wasn't the most worried outta all of us? 'Cept for maybe Joshua, who thinks you some kinda saint . . . and clearly does *not* know you like I do."

"Logan came around?"

Original Cindy nodded. "He came and yanked me outta my crib, and we haul butt to Terminal City, to see was you there, and guess what, you wasn't."

"What did he . . . ?"

"What'd he tell me? He tell me everything. You don't tell Original Cindy half a story, Boo—I'm like a priest, except for the religion part. Anyway, Logan come and found me and played me every track, includin' the bonus cuts—then he and me go out searchin' for your thoughtless self."

Max sat on the bench, embarrassed. "Jeez . . . I am

sorry. Really. I . . . when bad stuff happens, I kinda revert to, you know, a . . ."

"Selfish bitch?"

Max laughed. "Yeah. That's it exactly."

The lovely lesbian smiled and sat next to her. Taking one of the coffees, O.C. said, "Thanks, girl-friend—Original Cindy's gonna need the caffeine to get through this mother. You and me, we need to talk."

"I don't think I can take—"

"You gonna hide from this? Sooner or later you're gonna have to deal—better do it now, be done with it."

"I know," Max admitted. "Sorry about last night . . . just had to get away." She let out a long, tired breath. "Logan told you . . . everything?"

"You mean, do I know about Seth? Yeah. And I'm sorry for your loss, honey . . . which was two years ago, by the way."

"I know it's an old wound, but Logan ripped it wide open." Shaking her head, Max said, "I can't believe he *lied* to me."

Original Cindy snorted. "He can't help bein' a dick—you *got* a dick, sometimes you gon' *be* a dick."

"You got that right," Max said, laughing again, holding out her fist so O.C. could bump it, but the woman made no move to complete the ritual. "You gonna leave a sistah hangin'?"

Original Cindy's eyes went to the floor, then back to Max. "Only Logan, he ain't no all-the-time-a-dick, Max. He's human—made a mistake. But he's a good man . . . you know, for a man."

Max dropped her hand. "You're sticking up for him?"

"How many times you been in love, Boo?"

Max said nothing.

"Logan—he's the first, ain't he?"

Defensive, Max blurted, "I been around."

"I ain't talkin' about sex, sugah—we talkin' love. You *love* that four-eyed crip, don't ya?"

Max shrugged.

"And he loves your sorry mean ass."

Another shrug.

"Listen to Original Cindy. I been in love more times than . . . more times than I shoulda been. You think just 'cause somebody loves you that means they perfect? You think I ain't been lied to by somebody who loved me?"

"This isn't some . . . little white lie, Cindy."

"Don't play the race card, girl. Quit poutin' and get back in the game."

"What are you talking about?"

Original Cindy sighed. "Is Logan or is Logan not the single best dealio you ever run into in this whole sorry, solitary world? Present company excluded, of course."

That made Max smile. "Except for meeting you, Boo . . . yeah. I suppose. Logan's the best thing. Or anyway . . . he was."

"So. You gonna let one little slip ruin your whole life?"

"It was not a little slip," Max said, an edge in her voice. "Logan caused the death of my brother—and then he lied to me about it."

Normal appeared at the end of the aisle and said, "I

hate to interrupt this touching reunion, but I have a pressing delivery that—"

"Go away," Max snapped, and—simultaneously—Original Cindy shouted, "Not now, flat top! Can't you see we busy?"

Normal's eyes opened very wide. Then, instead of frowning or lashing back at them, Normal beamed. "Just like the good old days."

And Normal turned and walked away.

"You know," Original Cindy said with a smirk, digging a hole in one cheek, "I think I liked him better when he was a whole bastard. This halfa bastard, halfa nice guy shit . . . it's confusing."

That made Max smile . . .

. . . but only for a moment.

"Cindy, some things in a . . . relationship, you can't undo them. Some things just . . . cross the line."

"He didn't cheat on your ass or anything."

"Worse. Much worse."

"Excuse me? Is this Max who used to steal shit from people and peddle the goods to a fence? You remember her, right? . . . Perfect, faultless Max?"

"Cindy, he lied to me. If there's no trust—"

"He did not lie."

"He sure as hell did!"

"This is one of them, sins of *oh*-mission, as 'posed to sin of *co*-mission."

"I don't see the difference."

"The man did not lie. He just . . . kinda held back the truth."

"There's a word for that, Cindy."

". . . Bullshit?"

"No . . . sophistry." Her mentor Moody had taught her that.

"Sof' his'try, hard his'try . . . it should *be* history, you dig?"

"Some things can't be forgiven."

Original Cindy backed away and lifted her head and gazed down at Max, as if she were trying to see her better. "You look like Max and you sound like Max . . . but you can't be Max."

Not at all in the mood for being kidded, Max turned away from her friend.

" 'Cause if you was the real Max? You wouldn't be such a damn fool."

"Thank you very much."

"How long you known Logan?"

". . . Goin' on two years."

"And how much you been through together?"

". . . A lot."

"And who was always there for you no matter how bad things got?"

"You."

O.C. grinned. "Goes without sayin', but who else?"

"Joshua."

Original Cindy punched her lightly in the shoulder. "Thank you for makin' my point about you bein' a damn fool."

Max managed a tiny grin. "Logan has always been there. For me."

"Yeah. And that's somethin', ain't it, in this post-Pulse piece-of-shit world? . . . Who I got?"

"Well—you got me."

"Yeah, and hey, Boo, thass a lot, don't get me wrong,

but that ain't everything, you dig? Friendship is cool, way cool—but we got needs, you and me, that you and me don't do for each other."

Chuckling, Max admitted, "Yeah, I suppose."

Original Cindy was not chuckling. "Me, I had Diamond . . . only, she's gone."

Diamond Latrell had been Original Cindy's one true love, or so it seemed to Max; Latrell had been injected with a biotech experiment while in prison. Max helped Logan bring down Synthedyne, the corporation responsible for the experiments, and Diamond managed to pass the bioagent on to Synthedyne's CEO Sidney Croal before she, too, died.

"I know, Cin," Max said. "I'm so sorry. . . ."

"True love's a bitch, ain't it? To try an' find in this world, I mean . . . and you done found it, Boo. And 'cause your lover boy held back somethin', 'cause he was afraid it would hurt you and he didn't want to risk losin' you . . . 'cause he ain't perfect, you're ready to crumple that up and toss it away like a damn candy wrapper?"

"Cin . . . I can't trust him."

"Well, of course you can't," O.C. said, rolling her eyes. "He's a man, ain't he?"

"He's a man."

"Then sayin' you can't trust him is like sayin' water's wet. That's why the divorce rate is sixty-forty against, right?"

"I guess."

"But you can trust him for some things."

"Such as?"

Original Cindy took one of Max's hands in both of hers. "Trust that he's gonna love you till he dies."

". . . You think?"

She nodded. "Trust he's always got your back and ain't never gonna let nothin' bad happen to you, not if he can help it."

"Then why did he not tell me about Seth for all that time, only to spring it on me now?"

"You rather he never tell ya?"

". . . In a way."

"So it's okay for you to lie to yourself; it's just other people who can't lie to you. Boo, the man's tryin' to be honest. He knows he screwed up, and he was tryin' to fix it . . . not make it worse."

"But he did."

"Girl! You wanna pout till doomsday? Or you want a man in your life that couldn't take your fine ass to bed till he owned up with you 'bout something that was burnin' a hole in him? Boy's got a damn conscience, and you kicked him outta your life not for bein' dishonest . . . but for bein' *honest*!"

Stunned by Cindy's take on the situation, Max sat and quietly considered her friend's words.

Finally, she was starting to see this from outside herself. It would have been easy for Logan to keep up the lie—all he had to do was keep his mouth shut. She never would have found out about Seth if he hadn't told her . . .

"Don't you ever get tired of it?" Max asked Original Cindy.

"Tired of what?"

"Being right."

O.C. grinned and took a long drink from her coffee. "Oh, it's a burden, baby . . . Now, then—what you gonna do about this shit?"

That question was hard to answer.

Making a face, Original Cindy said, "That coffee's cold. Let's go get some fresh, and talk this sucker out."

Max shook her head.

"Why not?"

"I really think I've heard everything you have to say on this subject."

Worried, Original Cindy said, "That won't stop Original Cindy from houndin' you. You best give in."

"Know what? Think I 'best' go talk to Logan."

Original Cindy's face lit up. "Now you're talkin', Boo."

"I suppose I owe it to him to at least . . . *try* to straighten things out."

"See, girl? You ain't terminally infected with the bitch bug, after all! Maybe ol' Kelpy took that one on, too."

Max yelped a laugh and gently slugged her friend's arm.

O.C.'s smile melted into a frown.

"Oh," Max said. "Didn't mean to hit you hard or anything . . ."

"Ain't that, Boo. It's just . . . if you're finally goin' to see Logan, and we're not goin' out after fresh coffee . . . thass tragic in its own self."

"How so?"

"It means . . . Original Cindy's got to go to work."

They both laughed, and then they hugged.

Max felt a tear working its way down her cheek. As they broke, she hastily wiped it away.

But Cindy had caught the action, and said with the surprising gentleness this tough woman carried, "Don't worry, Boo. It's gonna work out. You two *both* too pretty to be unhappy."

"Oh, you," Max said, nodding and trying to smile, wanting to share her friend's confidence; but truth was, she held little hope.

There was that damned word again: hope.

And maybe this apprehension was why—on her way to see Logan—she stopped first at the control center in Terminal City. She told herself she was doing this out of a sense of responsibility, but she knew nonetheless that she might just be stalling.

Still, she hadn't spent this long a time out of touch with the others since the beginning of the siege. She was their leader, and it bothered her that she'd given so little thought to her responsibilities, that she had gone off by herself without consideration for her friends, who—like Original Cindy—had probably been worried about her.

The strange thing about last night was, she had enjoyed the time to herself, the solitude, even if she had been basking in something approaching self-pity. Within her the call of the maverick was struggling to be heard. She wondered if her life would always contain these contradictory urges, reflecting the periods when she'd been a part of a group . . . as at Manticore, or with the L.A. street gang, the Brood . . . and those other times when she'd been very much on her own, scratching for survival, based upon her own skills and wits.

Seattle had begun as a quest for anonymity—once Seth was lost to her, Max only wanted to blend in with the crowd, a loner on the watch for her Manticore pursuers. But over the course of two years, another family had gathered itself around her: Cindy and Joshua and Sketchy and Alec and the other transgenics, and even Normal, and, yes, most of all Logan.

Was the presence of this family a comforting one in her life, or merely smothering?

She passed through those tall forbidding gates, made the walk to the heavy steel door that led into the control center, the weight of that door seeming to transfer to her as she swung it open.

Made up of two distinct sections, upper and lower, the control center resembled electronics stores Max had seen in pre-Pulse vids and movies. The back section of the lower half was given over to a large layout table where the group held council sessions; right now it was largely covered by a map of Terminal City and the surrounding neighborhoods. The front section was a pyramid of video monitors, a dozen screens where four transgenics kept an eye on the local media and what the world out there was up to. Four stairs led to a raised level, where another thirteen monitors were pyramided, showing the Terminal City security system, both interior and the perimeter. From a command chair up there, Dix supervised the entire operation.

Down below, huddled over the map, Mole, Alec, and Joshua were in the midst of a powwow.

Mole was first to notice her return. "Hey, boss lady—where the hell you been?"

She tossed him a sarcastic smile. "Mr. Warmth—sweet to see you, too."

"Hey," Mole said, grinning, considering the appellation. "I think I like that—Mr. Warmth."

Max cheerfully flipped him off and asked, "Status?"

"Nice and quiet," he said. "Somehow we survived a night without you."

Joshua—just your average dog man in an army field jacket, T-shirt, and jeans—lumbered around the table and enveloped her in a bear hug. "Little Fella!"

His silly yet somehow endearing nickname for her gave Max a sudden rush of warmth.

Also, she was struggling to keep breathing—the transgenic's fondness for her was exceeded only by his grasp.

Squeezing out words like the last smidgens from a toothpaste tube, Max managed, "Heeey . . . Big Fella. What's shaking?"

Joshua released her from his crushing embrace, and the noble, shaggy face studied her. "*Joshua* was shaking, till now. Now that I see Max is all right."

"Sorry to worry you," she said, meaning it. "I had to think about some stuff."

Suddenly Alec was at her side. As usual, the X5's attire seemed parked halfway between beach boy and biker, a gray leather jacket over a T-shirt and dark jeans. "Logan told us about Seth."

Max couldn't read the handsome face, and asked, "So how do you feel about it?"

"Logan recruiting Seth?"

"Logan recruiting Seth and getting him killed."

Alec half smirked. "Come on, Max—Seth musta got *himself* killed. He was one impulsive dude, right? Anyway, he was a big boy—he knew the game and he knew the stakes."

"What about Logan lying to us?"

Alec grunted something that might have been a laugh. "Oh yeah, I'm pretty worked up about that. I mean, I never lied to anyone, my whole life, right? . . . And I'm sure you've been straight with Logan, hundred percent, since day one."

That made her flinch a little, but she managed to cover.

Of course she'd lied to Logan—plenty of times, since they'd met; in the early days particularly, before trust had been built up. But this was different—this mattered; this had been about something important. Yet the sense that she was guilty of judging by a double standard burned in her stomach.

Max said, "You guys seem to've got by fine without me last night."

"Well, you sent us on a merry chase," Alec said. "But yeah—Terminal City stands in all its glory."

"Can you guys get by without me awhile longer?"

Alec shrugged. "Girl's gotta do what a girl's gotta do."

From the sidelines, Mole pitched in: "We'll be fine, Max. Take some time. Chill."

Alec's smirk widened. "Like you're capable of chilling."

She ignored that.

"Okay then," she said to the group. "I'll be at Logan's for a while, you need me."

Joshua said, "Logan is a good man, Max. Don't be mad at him."

"Or at least be fair and make sure he's wearin' that exoskeleton thingie," Alec said. "You know . . . 'fore you kick his ass?"

She shook her head, but couldn't hold back the smile. "You're bad, Alec. Truly bad."

"That's the rumor," he said.

Almost at a run, she took the tunnel between the two former Medtronics buildings, the one inside the Terminal City fencing and the one on the other side. Logan owned both buildings in the name of a fictional company, Sowley Opticals. Even though the siege was over and she could use the streets, the private passage of the tunnel felt more comfortable.

The tunnel had concrete walls and ceiling, and a tile floor, all a dull hospital green; fluorescent lights hung every thirty feet or so. Her boots were almost silent on the floor and Max stayed quiet, keeping her breathing shallow as she strolled toward the far end. She liked the silence down here—sometimes so still, she could hear her own blood coursing through her veins.

Going up the stairs at the far end, she could see a slice of light from Logan's apartment around the door, which was partially open—usually, it would be closed and locked, and she wondered if Logan had company.

That would be perfect: here she was ready to try to forgive him, and on the other side of that door, he's crying on some other girl's shoulder—Asha, maybe . . .

As she reached for the knob, shaking off her lover's paranoia, she could detect voices in there; but this wasn't Logan's voice, nor Asha's for that matter— these voices spoke something that wasn't even English . . .

Not convinced anything was wrong—but hardly ready to cheerfully call out, "Anybody home?"—she stepped quickly, quietly inside . . .

. . . and saw a man with a gun.

A squat Latino with a buzz cut and a dour, puffy face, Logan's "guest" wore jeans and a black T-shirt and no coat, despite the bitter cold outside; an F was tattooed on the man's right forearm, the branches of the letter formed from forearms and clenched fists. He held an Uzi loosely in both hands.

The tattoo marked the visitor as a member of the Furies, a gang from Sector Eight—a guest who would hardly be stopping by Logan's to sing Christmas carols. The Furies considered themselves the badasses to end all badasses, but in Max's opinion these Latinos ruled Sector Eight by sheer strength of numbers.

With over a hundred soldiers in their ranks, the Furies were broken up into units of ten—"packs," which tended to include specialists in arson, theft, torture, sniping, and various other skills, making each little unit self-contained for assorted fun and games.

If the asshole with the Uzi was here, she knew the rest of his pack wasn't far away. Logan not in sight, she stood alone, here—which made the likely odds at least ten to one. She considered going back for

Joshua and the others, and she could have outrun these clowns and ducked their bullets, or maybe she could just slip back out and use her cell to bring the gang running, yeah, that would be the smart move . . .

. . . only the guy heard or sensed her now, and his flat-featured face lifted to scowl at her.

He grunted, and it might have turned into a word, but that was all the sound he got out before Max took two swift steps and leapt as he brought up the gun, way too late. Her foot connected with his throat and he toppled over, crashing to the floor, the Uzi bouncing away—fortunately not firing, though making enough of a clatter to attract Logan's other "guests" . . .

Furies appeared from everywhere—they'd spread out through the apartment—and she took a tally, even as she started dispatching the gang members.

Soon she realized that two full packs filled Logan's digs! Twenty-to-one odds were a hell of a handful for even someone as skilled as Max . . .

She was a dervish, though, kicking this one, sweeping the feet out from that one, punching a third to the floor. The odds didn't matter—fighting through these invaders and locating Logan were her only goals now. It didn't matter that he'd lied about Seth, or that they'd had a spat, nothing mattered but getting to him . . . and his being alive.

She kicked one Fury in the groin, and he went down howling as two more converged on her, from behind; she leaned back, grabbed each of them by the back of the skull and slammed them together face first. They dropped in a bloody, silent heap, their faces smears of red that seemed if anything an improvement.

That was when she saw Logan, five Furies on him like army ants, dragging him from the bedroom toward the front door.

What the hell?

What did a street gang have to gain by kidnapping Logan?

She jumped, kicking to either side, each foot connecting with the head of a Fury, sending both bangers to a dark place. As they fell, she landed nimbly, then turned toward the five Furies who had hauled the struggling Logan to the door.

Logan spotted her and yelled her name—and in the sound of his voice there were myriad emotions, from fear to regret, and love was in there, too.

But she could do nothing—there were too many of the bastards—and that she was still kicking ass when the five dragged Logan out into the bright sunshine of the frigid morning provided no damn solace at all.

Time was key—seconds could mean life or death. She punched the nearest one and wrenched the weapon from his hands, a small submachine gun. She hated guns and had vowed years ago that she would never use one, but she needed to save Logan and— filled with revulsion as she was—this seemed the only way to even the odds.

She jerked back the bolt on the weapon, but before she could fire, a Buddha bunch of arms closed over and around her and she found herself wrestling with half a dozen Furies for control of the weapon. They weren't stronger than her, not hardly; but there were just so goddamn many of them!

Finally, she released the Uzi and returned to the hand-to-hand combat at which she excelled. Besides, the Furies were loyal, a family however dysfunctional, and if she stayed in close, they wouldn't dare fire automatic weapons into a crowd of their cronies.

She hadn't, however, seen the Tazer.

The two prongs dug into her back, and she knew instantly what had happened, even before the violent shaking started and the thought of reaching Logan was driven from her mind by the searing pain that consumed every cell of her being as she did a macabre marionette's dance at the end of the two wires feeding voltage into her back.

She tried to fall but couldn't, the electricity holding her up until all the Furies had exited the building, the one controlling the Tazer leaving last. She vibrated for a second more, then dropped over, unconscious.

Max awoke with a violent start, the smell of ammonia filling her nostrils. "Wha . . . what . . . *Logan*! They got Logan!"

A hand rested on her shoulder, and she turned, drawing reflexively back to punch, pulling it as she looked up into the reptilian face of Mole.

"It's okay," he said. "It's me."

"They got him! They got Logan!"

"Easy—settle," Mole said.

She looked around now to see that Alec, Joshua, and a couple of X3s she didn't recognize were combing the apartment. The Furies had cleaned up their wounded and taken them along, too. She took some small satisfaction knowing that she had inflicted a good deal of damage on them; grabbing Logan hadn't come free for the sons of bitches.

Mole helped her into a kitchen chair. "How'd you know to come?" she asked, her body a mass of pains, her head pounding to an unseen but insistent drumbeat.

"Luke," he said, referring to Dix's lightbulb-headed best buddy. "He was going out for supplies when he saw a bunch of bangers pilin' into a truck and taking off. He figured that couldn't be good, called us."

"The Furies," she said. "They took Logan."

Alec walked in holding a piece of black T-shirt. "Looks like their 'uniform.' What the hell would those idiots want with Logan?"

They all took turns looking at each other and shrugging.

"Logan's rich, isn't he?" Mole asked. "Maybe it's a snatch job. Anybody see a ransom note?"

No one had.

"They're organized," Alec said, sitting on the table near Max, "but I didn't think they were organized enough to manage something like this."

"Where's their HQ, anyway?" Mole asked. "Let's just go snatch him back."

Max shook her head. "I doubt that even the Furies are stupid enough to keep him at their crib. If they saw us coming, they might just kill him and run."

Mole frowned. "Well, what the hell do you suggest, then?"

"Don't know yet," Max said, still groggy.

Alec said, "Well, I do."

Max looked up at him.

"Leave it to me," he said.

Any idea was better than what she had—nothing—but the typical smugness in Alec's tone made Max think "leaving it to him" wasn't a wise strategy.

During the siege, trying to help, Alec and Joshua had nearly gotten themselves killed, been captured by Ames White, and almost singlehandedly destroyed any opportunity the transgenics had for a negotiated peace with the ordinaries. That was the most recent example of "leaving it to Alec" . . .

On the other hand, Alec seemed to have changed in recent months, and for the better. The new Alec had actually become a valuable member of the community, even of her inner council. He was considered by many the likeliest choice to run for the city council seat that would become Terminal City's official voice in Seattle politics.

That was the "new" Alec. But the gleam in Alec's eye suggested the old Alec was back in town, and that was almost as troubling as anything the Furies might manage.

"We won't be leaving this to you, Alec," she said.

"No?"

"No, but I'm ready to hear you out."

"You won't regret it," Alec said, flashing that smile, and he hopped off the table and pulled up the chair next to her, and she heard what he had in mind and, hardly believing it herself, found herself going along with him.

Chapter Five
SMART ALEC

SEATTLE, WASHINGTON
DECEMBER 21, 2021

Alec's plan had merit.

Just the same, Max—finally shaking off the shock of Logan's abduction, not to mention the aftereffects of the Tazer—had a plan of her own in mind.

And between the two of them, she thought, they might just be able to get Logan back alive.

She and Alec sat at the kitchen table in Logan's apartment and discussed their respective approaches. All of them—the other Terminal City insiders who were joining them in their efforts, Joshua, Dix, Mole—had come to feel that the kidnapping had an economic motive.

It was an easy enough conclusion to reach. Kidnapping for ransom had been around since the beginning of time, of course, but it had really made a splash in a post-Pulse United States, where money was hard to come by and even harder to hang onto. That made the privileged few, the wealthy who'd been largely untouched by the Pulse, prey to predators like the Furies.

Which meant that at some point a ransom note would be delivered, or a call or an e-mail would come in.

"If they were smart," Alec said, "they'd have snatched *you*, Max."

"You think they coulda managed that?"

"Why? Would you have argued with 'em, while you were doin' that Tazer dance?"

This was a good point, but she didn't acknowledge it, saying, "Why am I a better kidnap choice than Logan?"

"Logan's the one with the money. You kids don't exactly have a joint checking account yet, do you?"

This, too, was a good point.

Max said, "We don't have any way of tapping into Logan's coffers . . . not unless we can hack into various banks or somethin'."

"Which is where you come in," Alec said.

While Alec put his plan into action, Max would contact Logan's family in hopes of gaining their financial assistance. She only hoped the Cales would still be capable of coming up with the cash for whatever undoubtedly lunatic ransom demand the street gang would make.

The Cale family's money woes had begun in earnest when Logan's uncle Jonas was gunned down by a hoverdrone programmed by Jonas's business partner, Gilbert Neal. The deal that Neal had made after he killed Jonas cost the family millions; fortunately, Jonas wasn't the only rich Cale in the clan.

Logan's uncle Lyman—a legendary reclusive billionaire who was often compared by the media to that twentieth-century fruitcake moneybags, Howard Hughes—lived in a compound on Sunrise Island, a private island in Puget Sound. All Max knew about the eccentric uncle was that he was estranged from the rest of the family, with one significant exception: he was said to love his nephew, Logan. Logan rarely talked about him, though Max sensed that the two of them got along very well.

The media also reported that Lyman Cale's estate had cutting-edge high-tech high security. And Max knew it wasn't like she could let the old boy know she was coming to call. Wasn't like Lyman Cale was listed in the white pages . . . and Logan's computer was so encrypted that not even the cyberadept Dix could make a dent in it.

That meant she would simply have to flex her old cat-burglar muscles to get inside Uncle Lyman's compound and have a friendly chat with him about his favorite (and kidnapped) nephew. The prospect worried her not a whit—she'd had a good teacher in Moody, back in L.A. . . . Few could rival her breaking-and-entering skills.

While she was doing that, Alec would be infiltrating the Furies.

"I know those guys," he said. "Used to run into 'em, in certain parts of town, back when I worked at Jam Pony. They were always tryin' to recruit me."

"Isn't everybody?" she said with a faint smile.

"It's a gift," he said, returning the smile.

Seemed to Max that Alec thought everybody

wanted him for everything. He appeared certain that all women wanted to jump his bones and all men longed to be like him. It was a small world he lived in, but he was happy there.

"Maybe it's a little late in the game," Alec said, "but I figure I can look those bros up, and tell 'em I've finally come to my senses and realize the only future for me is as a Fury."

Such was Alec's plan—not very complicated, especially by Alec's Machiavellian standards, though the element of egomania marked it as his.

Barely sixty minutes had passed since the abduction, and they were ready to roll. It did not warm her within that she would have to trust Alec; she'd just found out that the steadfast, dependable person she figured she could trust the most in the world had lied to her—and now she was putting her faith in a handsome congenital liar.

And while Alec could go out and work the streets immediately, she would have to wait for nightfall to see Logan's uncle. Good as she was, like most cat burglars—most cats, for that matter—she was at her best under the cover of darkness.

She thought back on the estate of Jared Sterling, the computer billionaire she'd had a run-in with when she first got to Seattle. Sterling's estate had boasted state of the art security and she'd cracked that, hadn't she? Of course, she'd also been caught and had to kick the asses of four armed men, just to jump the fence again with her skin intact; but she had gotten in. Could Lyman Cale's estate be any tougher?

Probably.

So Max decided the best thing she could do in the daylight was some research on what awaited her on Sunrise Island.

As she and Alec rose from the table, each to pursue a plan, Alec looked at her with something akin to sympathy.

"I gotta hand it to you, Max—you're taking this well."

"Logan's not in any danger, not immediately—he's too valuable."

An atypically grave expression took over the handsome face. "Max . . . I hate to say this, but . . . in a certain number of cases like this, the kidnappers just ice the victim right outta the chutes. A lot of people have paid ransom money for a corpse."

"You're saying this why?"

"You just need to face that."

"If he's dead, what can I do about it? If he's alive, we'll get him back."

Alec nodded, smirked humorlessly. "I *thought* you were just holdin' it in . . . Anyway, I kinda got a hunch what you'll do about it, if he is dead. Just remember, I'm not really a Fury, okay?"

And he gave her that cocky grin.

Max smiled a little and nodded. Probably were quite a few females who wanted to jump those bones, at that . . .

And the deadly government-trained killing machine, the female X5 who knew a thousand ways to destroy her enemies, sprang into action—heading to Logan's computers, to do research.

•   •   •

Alec cruised his motorcycle on up to the checkpoint at Sector Eight. Trying to blend in, he wore a black ensemble of jeans, a turtleneck sweater, and a leather jacket. He flashed his old Jam Pony ID, held up an envelope he'd stuffed with old newspaper clippings, and got waved through by the sector guard who was too busy with the long line of pedestrians to pay much heed to a pain-in-the-ass messenger.

What with the difficulty of passing from sector to sector, and with gas so high and the streets and highways in such wretched shape, many businesses used services like Jam Pony, which meant the sector guards found messengers an all-too-common annoyance, and had a nice habit—nice from Alec's point of view, anyway—of just waving 'em through.

As he accelerated out of the checkpoint, Alec kissed the Jam Pony ID. This had been the easy part, he told himself; he'd only needed to be a little bit lucky. No time to get cocky. Getting into Sector Eight? A snap. Finding the information he needed and getting back out alive? A whole 'nother deal.

Sector Eight—tired and old and tucked beneath Portage Bay—served as the base of ops for several street gangs, and the Seattle P.D. seldom ventured far beyond the checkpoints. This far north, the shabby urban landscape provided lots of places to stash a body out of the way of prying eyes, official or otherwise.

The Furies operated out of Lakeview Cemetery and Volunteer Park, but had also been known to frequent the woods around Interlaken Boulevard and the Broadmoor. Once a very popular golf course, the

Broadmoor now housed a good-sized Jamestown that provided plenty of potential victims for the ruthless violence of the Furies.

Alec knew the Furies manned an observation station atop the Volunteer Park water tower. So this seemed as good a place as any to start. Not at all surreptitious, a man clearly confident about who he was and what he was doing, he rode into the woods, and then, not far from the tower, parked his cycle and strolled forward to within twenty yards of the building.

The tower was four squat stories of faded red brick, rising through the trees like a huge fat chimney, topped by a conical roof perched there like a Chinese farmer's bamboo hat. The structure seemed vaguely medieval to Alec, as he drew closer, though the historical edge was taken off by black spray-painted Furies graffiti.

Within the brick facade, a giant metal tank had at one time been filled with water. Talk now was, the tank was piled with the bodies of those who got in the way of the Furies. Alec figured this was an urban legend—after all, the only smell was of pine trees—but nonetheless he didn't know anyone who had been brave enough to go find out for themselves.

The way—a white, recessed door also adorned with Furies graffiti—was guarded by a pair of the bangers. In broad daylight, Alec saw only one way to do this: walk up like you own the place. It wasn't a foreign approach to the X5.

He stepped out of the woods and walked straight at the two guards, who wore black T-shirts and jeans, like all Furies. They were small for guards—maybe that was why there were two of them he thought—both about the same height, a good four inches shorter than he was, and stick-skinny. They didn't appear terribly bright, either—both looked to be on the dim side of forty watts.

Alec smiled as he approached, nodding, waving casually, and the two guards looked at each other, as if each hoped the other might have managed to form a thought. Then the same thought formed in both their limited minds, as they simultaneously pulled pistols from the waistbands of their pants and leveled them at Alec.

The guy on the left had a revolver which had probably last been fired before the Pulse, the one on the right brandishing a small caliber automatic that belonged in an old lady's handbag.

Pitiful. The only thing that made the Furies formidable was their numbers—they were the largest gang in Seattle, a mix of Latinos and Russians, mostly.

"Whoa whoa whoa," Alec said, his hands rising easily in a gesture of surrender, his smile never wavering. "I'm a friend, fellas . . . you know Manny?"

This was one of the two Furies he'd met a year or so ago and spent some time with, drinking beers they'd paid for when they were trying to recruit him.

"Manny not here," the one on the left said.

"Manny not here," echoed the one on the right. "You see Manny here?"

"I would have to agree," Alec said. "Manny not here—*where* Manny?"

The one on the left sighed heavily. *"Manny not here!"*

If he didn't find somebody smarter than a footstool to deal with soon, this was going to be a lot harder than he'd thought.

"How about Stefan?" he tried, dropping the name of the other Fury he knew.

The two guards looked at each other again, then returned their thick gaze to Alec.

"Stefan not here," one of them said, and that was it, Alec was fed up with these two. Another minute with them and there was no telling what kind of permanent damage he might do to his own IQ.

One more question, any question, should be all he'd need. He asked, "You two related?"

When they looked at each other this time, Alec plucked the guns from their hands, in a two-handed move, and flipped the pistols around so they were pointing at the guards, who gazed at him with eyes and mouths open.

"This is where you put your hands up," he advised the pair.

Four hands shot skyward.

"Good, fellas. Nice reflexes."

The one on the left turned to the one on the right. "You screwed up."

"*I* screwed up?"

His brain hurting, Alec said, "Shut up and turn around."

They did, facing the tower now.

"This is stupid," the one on the left said to Alec, "what you're doin'."

"Well," Alec said cheerfully, "you'd know."

And—in another two-handed move—smacked them both on the back of the head with the gun butts. Firmly. Both guards dropped to the sidewalk with little sound, a couple of skinny piles of kindling.

Alec tucked the guns in his waistband, then dragged the two guards, one at a time, into the underbrush. He tied them up, using their own belts and shirts, then returned to the now unguarded door.

It opened in on a white metal stairwell, the only light provided by the sun glinting through the doorway. On his left was the gray, riveted body of the metal tank, which might have once been white, but time and lack of care had bruised it gray, more Furies graffiti decorating it.

The stairs circled the tank and led up into darkness. Alec had no clue how many Furies were up there; however many, there was bound to be at least one smarter than the bonehead guards. He had a miniflash in his pocket and considered using it, only he didn't want to give away his position, so it stayed put.

The X5 had abandoned his like-he-owned-the-place approach; now that he'd taken those guards out, he was officially an invader, trying to maintain silence as he crept up the steps. His rubber-soled shoes made no noise and he kept his breathing relaxed and regular.

After four minutes and over one hundred stairs, Alec came around a turn into light—the entrance to the observation deck must've been standing wide open. This didn't surprise him; the Furies were probably up and down these stairs all the time. They had guards posted downstairs, didn't they?

At the top of the stairs, Alec plastered himself to the wall and gazed through the open doorway.

The floor was concrete, the brick, occasionally graffitied walls punctuated every eight feet or so by arched openings, which may at one time have been glassed-in windows but now stood open to the weather. The gray bulk of the inner tower made the observation deck a relatively narrow glorified covered walkway that curved around.

At the third window down from where Alec watched, three Furies sat in a sandbag bunker. One Fury took a turn as sentry at a window, using binoculars—but not in the direction Alec had come, luckily; the other two bangers were playing cards and good-naturedly bitching at each other about the game.

The one with the binoculars looked to be in his early twenties, with dark hair, another Latino; like the rest of the Furies, he wore a black T-shirt and blue jeans—it wasn't much of a uniform but it was theirs. The card player on the left was a big, heavy guy with long, stringy dark hair and a middle European look. Brushing bangs out of his eyes, he said, "C'mon, Hutt, play a damn card."

"Jack of spades," Hutt said triumphantly as he dropped the card on the pile. He was thinner than his opponent, but his hair was the same dark, stringy mess, and he had a similar ethnic cast—the cardplayers might be brothers.

"Ha," the fat one said, snapping up the card.

"Think you got the winning hand there, pal?" Alec asked.

At the sound of the unfamiliar voice, the fat guy looked up; none of the trio had heard the stranger's approach. "Huh?"

Alec's casualness froze the three dopes.

"I like my hand better," the X5 said.

And he swung his right fist, connecting with the side of the fat guy's head. The fat guy's eyes rolled back, he wobbled for a second as cards filtered out of his hands, then he just fell over on his side, unconscious.

Hutt had already started to rise, but Alec's spinning kick dropped him, cold.

The sentry, facing Alec now, hurled the binoculars, but Alec ducked the throw and stepped forward, his hand closing over the guy's windpipe.

"Hey," Alec said. "I'm a guest."

The guy wasn't much more than a kid himself, maybe twenty, zits covering his face, his eyes bloodshot, his skin the color of wet newspaper. He squeaked but that was all he could get out, and when Alec increased the pressure, the squeak turned to silence.

The idea—a quick revision of his plan, now that joining up with the Furies seemed less likely—was to squeeze info out of the sentry, find out where Logan was . . .

Then Alec saw something that hadn't been apparent from the doorway—off to the left, around the concealing curve of the inner tower, was a second sandbag bunker, six windows away, with three more

Furies, two of whom were rushing toward him and his captive, the third furiously punching numbers on a cell phone.

The sentry Alex held by the neck became suddenly useless, and the X5 popped him with a straight right. The guy pitched onto the sandbags and took a nap. Finding out Logan's whereabouts had become secondary to survival.

The bangers running up to him spread out, so despite the relatively closed-in area, Alec couldn't get them both at once—unlike the guards below, these two weren't complete morons . . . unfortunately. The one to his left—a stocky Latino—came in with a long, looping right that Alec ducked, and countered with a right that caught the guy in the solar plexus, air bursting out of the Fury as his body slapped to the cement.

The second one, a burly Russian, pulled a knife and advanced, waving the blade back and forth. Presumably this had intimidated opponents in the past; Alec disarmed the guy, just slapping the blade from his grasp, and caught him on the chin with a left hook that sent him down for the count . . . a long count.

The one with the cell phone, a medium-sized blond guy with short hair and light blue eyes, took one look at the wreckage of his friends and flew off running in the other direction. Must've been stairs around that way, too . . .

But he had already done his damage: his cell phone call had summoned the troops—feet were pounding up the nearer stairs, a small army headed toward the observation deck, a metallic echoing too much like machine-gun fire for Alec's taste. An X5 was first and foremost a soldier, and Alec knew all about when it was time to retreat. He went to one of the archway windows.

The four-story drop was just too far to risk, even for a transgenic. So he stood on the ledge and gripped the edge of the Chinese-hat tile roof; he might be able to perch up there and wait it out until the reinforcements left. As if doing a pull-up, he clambered up and lay against the roof, just listening to the show within the observation deck.

The first voice he heard, he recognized: Manny, the Fury he'd met almost a year ago.

"Christ," Manny said. "What went on up here? Hutt doin' crank again?"

"From what I heard on the cell," someone else said excitedly, "it was one guy—all over everybody! Who the fuck can fight like that?"

The next voice was cooler, more in control, probably the guy in charge. "Stefan, you and Woodrow secure the far end."

"Yes, Badar," Stefan said. This voice Alec recognized, too—a pity Stefan and Manny hadn't been around when he came calling; this wouldn't have played out so bad . . .

On the other hand, he had struck a sort of gold.

Badar, he knew, would be Badar Tremaine, leader of the Furies and generally considered the biggest badass for three sectors. Alec had never spoken to the gang leader, but had seen him around, and like most everybody else in Seattle, he'd heard plenty about him—tall, slender, with black hair usually swept back in a tight ponytail, Tremaine had close-set dark eyes, a perpetual stubble, and skin the color of oiled leather.

The good news was that Badar undoubtedly would have either approved or masterminded the Logan Cale kidnapping. Alec clung to the edge of the roof, hanging over a bit, listening intently.

He heard four feet pounding down the observation deck toward the far end.

"Savage!" Tremaine again. "You and Dante guard the stairs at this end. Make sure the deck is secure."

Again Alec heard two men run back to the door. The wind was whipping at him, and ruffling the nearby trees; but his transgenic hearing stood him in good stead. He was in a decent position up here, as long as no Fury below saw him, clinging to the roof in broad daylight.

That would be . . . unfortunate.

"Manny, this is just the sort of setback we don't need right now."

"I know, Badar."

"Sounds like maybe it's one of Cale's transgenic friends dropped by . . . Hit the woods, scour the area, check the Jamestown. Find the bastard who did this."

"And bring him to you?"

"Just kill him."

"You got it, Badar."

"Don't screw it up! Nothing can interfere with our plans—Cale's worth too much to us. The ransom note has been sent, but you can't trust these transgenics. What we had up here may be their idea of paying up . . . God only knows if these mutant freaks even understand the concept of money."

Alec fought the urge to swing over the rail and kick the crap out of Badar Tremaine.

"If everything remains on schedule tonight," Tremaine was saying, "I want you to move Cale first thing in the morning."

"The troll?" Manny asked.

"Yeah."

The troll? Who the hell was the troll? Alec wondered. Was that some bizarre reference to Logan?

"Everything's secure, Badar." Stefan's voice again. "There's no sign of who did this, but we found one of the sentries hiding on the back stairs."

"Bring him to me."

Alec quickly thought his situation through: the blond sentry, the cell-phone caller who'd summoned the troops, had been on the back stairs. Badar and his Furies had come up the other stairs—soon they would figure out that their intruder hadn't gone down either of those stairways, hence could only have gone out a window . . .

He looked down and decided again that trying to land safely from this height was a really bad idea. He could swing in and take on the room of gangbangers, but if they captured him, or killed him, what he'd heard would go unreported to Max.

Even if he prevailed, the other Furies might simply kill Logan, rather than risk another confrontation.

The wind whispered to him, through the sun-shimmering leaves.

Alec heard them.

Picking out the nearest, tallest pine tree, he jumped.

Sunrise Island, site of Lyman Cale's compound, was just east of Vashon Island in the sound, and a boat could be launched from Three Tree Point. The ride to Sunrise would be shortest at that point—less than half an hour—though, after that, things got a little hairier: Max figured on electric fences, dogs, guns, security staff, the whole nine booby-trapped yards.

She wasn't looking forward to the trip, but Dix hadn't come up with any other ways of contacting the old man. Jonas Cale's older brother, Lyman, had made his money years ago and controlled a massive bank account that was separate even from the formidable wealth of the Cale family money.

Max found a recent online video of Lyman addressing Congress from his compound. A world class recluse, the old man hadn't set foot on the mainland since the Pulse. In the video, as he droned on about "the need for economic opportunity in this climate of fiscal unease," he gave the appearance of a vibrant older man. Silver-haired with a distinguished spade-shaped white beard, he revealed flashing blue eyes that reminded Max of Logan's, and a short straight nose over a wide, thin-lipped mouth.

The old boy certainly wasn't half bad to look at; she wondered if she were possibly viewing a snapshot of Logan at that age. That such a thought would form again, unbidden, was a positive sign . . . Maybe she was getting past the Seth thing. Maybe Logan Cale was worth growing old with, after all.

Assuming he wasn't already dead . . .

Dusk was deepening to night and they hadn't heard from Alec yet; she couldn't wait any longer. The ransom note had shown up at Terminal City early this afternoon—delivered by a Jam Pony messenger, no less—and Max now knew the depth of their trouble. The message—addressed to Max, boldly, arrogantly signed "The Furies"—said that if she didn't bring $4 million to Gas Works Park tomorrow at dawn, Logan would die.

It troubled Max that the note had been addressed to her—they knew of her friendship with Logan, knew it ran deep enough to convince them she could raise this fortune, either from the Cole family or by Logan trusting her with his finances.

Four million or forty million, what was the difference? Without Lyman Cale, she had no chance of saving Logan. His cousin Bennett—now in charge of Jonas's millions—would just as soon see Logan dead as alive. At least Jonas had liked having Logan around just to have someone to persecute; Bennett didn't even care enough about Logan to hate him—all Bennett knew was one less cousin meant a larger stake for him, when the Jonas Cale fortune eventually got split up.

The night was clear but cold as Max eased the "borrowed" boat out into the water. She was amazed at how easily she slipped back into her old ways. Telling herself that it was for Logan helped muffle the micron of guilt, but in truth she felt comfortable in the role Moody had schooled her in. In some dark part of her, it felt good, breaking the rules again.

The borrowed boat had a big outboard; while she didn't know much about the difference between boat motors, she was well-acquainted with the concept of "bigger means faster." Manticore had also trained her to operate most any motorized vehicle, so racing across Puget Sound in someone else's speedboat was no prob.

The sound lay quiet and glassy smooth, and Max's new toy skimmed along the surface at just over thirty miles per hour. That might be too fast, given that it was dark and she didn't know for sure what lay in her path; but she was anxious to make contact with the elder Cale, and the thought of Logan's dilemma drove her mercilessly.

So she dropped the hammer and roared through the night. The moon was a big bright white ball, a hole in the sky letting in light that made this leg of the journey easy; but it would provide more illumination than she would want, on landing.

Still a mile away, she cut the engine, anchored the speedboat, and took a smaller rubber raft the rest of the way. Dragging the raft up onto the shore, she was surprised that there seemed to be no walls around Lyman Cale's compound. The old man owned the whole island, and the mansion and two guest houses were the only ones on the tiny private piece of land. A massive forest made up the perimeter, but she knew—from her net research—the mansion sat in the middle.

Slow-scanning the woods in front of her, she looked for lasers, electronic eyes, dogs, anything . . . and found nothing. Moving carefully, she started inland. By her estimate, she was only about a quarter mile from the big house when she saw the first hint of security—a guard dressed in black leading a Doberman around the perimeter. The guard had on TAC team fatigues, including a balaclava that covered most of his face and a Kevlar vest, and he carried an automatic weapon that hung loosely from his right shoulder.

Max's enhanced night vision gave her an advantage over both man and beast, but when the dog's nose went into the air, and the animal's head cocked in her direction, she knew she had trouble.

"What is it, boy?" the guard asked.

The guard was about to key the mike attached to the left shoulder of his uniform when Max put on a burst of speed and outflanked the pair. She came right up behind the guard, tapped him on the shoulder, and when he turned, she smiled pleasantly at him.

This unexpected behavior coming from an attractive young woman froze the guard, and he said only, "Huh?"

Or at least that was all he got out before she kicked him in the groin, a dry heave of pain groaning up out of him as he doubled over: Before that groan could turn into something louder, Max delivered an uppercut that lifted the man off his feet and deposited him in an unconscious heap next to the surprised dog, which had backed up at this blur of movement.

Now, however, baring its teeth, the Doberman prepared to launch itself at Max; before it could, however, she yanked a baseball-size hunk of hamburger from her pocket and lobbed it to the dog, who caught it in mid-flight, swallowed the thing practically whole. Chewing, licking his chops, the creature took a menacing step toward her, eyeing her—giving Max a chance to toss him some more burger before taking care of business.

The Doberman made several slow threatening steps her way when it began to wobble, went glassy-eyed, then dropped onto its stomach, as if the urge for a nap had overridden everything.

Which it had.

The Doberman began to snore as Max bent over the prone figure of the guard. The pill in the center of the hamburger had been a concoction courtesy of Luke, who had promised that the dog would be having happy puppy dreams for the rest of the night, no harm, no foul. That was good, because Max preferred not to harm animals, with the occasional exception of humans.

Of course, hamburger—any meat, for that matter—was a black market extravagance in today's third world economy; still, Max felt this had been money well spent. "Stuff costs an arm and a leg," a protesting Dix had said. Maybe so, but—from the look of that slumbering Doberman—thanks to Luke, at least the limbs lost tonight weren't hers.

She lifted the guard's radio and clipped the mike to her own shoulder; couldn't hurt for her to hear what was going on around her.

Continuing on, she repeated the procedure with three more perimeter teams, her kicks taking out the guards, Luke's special meatballs downing the dogs. She had just taken out the fourth—and what she figured to be the final outside man-and-dog guard team—when the radio crackled to life.

"Post One—report."

Max said nothing—even if she'd known what to say, her unfamiliar female voice would have sent up a red flag. Knowing full well "Post One" was not going to be answering his page anytime soon, she approached the big house, a three-story replica of a plantation mansion out of the Civil War South. Though she'd never been east of the Mississippi in her life, Max had received Manticore training that included segments on Sherman's march to the sea, with an emphasis on the folly of pitched battles such as Gettysburg; so she recognized an antebellum mansion when she saw one.

"Post One—report! Johnson, you there?"

Only silence greeted the dispatcher.

"Post Two, check on Post One . . . Post Two?"

More crackly silence.

She heard the dispatcher mutter, *"What the hell?"* Then a fire-type clanging alarm went off and light flooded the yard from the top of every building.

Max ducked into a hedge near the front door, getting out of sight. The lights had turned the front lawn into instant noon. She peeked out from the bushes to see half a dozen security men come pouring out the front door. The first four looked like your average rent-a-goons, but the last two were broad-shouldered, muscular paramilitary types. Both had close-cropped hair, one blond, one brown, and wore TAC fatigues like the others, only on these guys the clothes looked different, as if they knew what all the nasty toys were for. The clanging alarm stopped as they took off toward the water, running in two-man combat formation. By comparison, the rest of the crew seemed to be auditioning for a Chinese fire drill.

As the last of the guards disappeared into the darkness, Max came out from behind the hedge, slipped through the door, closed it and locked it. That wouldn't keep the guards out for long, but she didn't need long—she just needed to get past this insulation and locate Lyman Cale and explain the situation. Though Logan had said little about his uncle, what she'd heard was positive, and she just knew he would want to help.

The first floor of the house was not what she expected at all—no furniture in the entry way, the living room, or the den on the opposite side. Except where security teams had walked, a patina of dust covered the floor, and it looked like no one had cleaned the place in years.

In fact, it looked like no one had *lived* here in years.

As she made her way up the wide stairs to the second floor, Max listened carefully, hearing no one, nothing. Then, at the far end of the hall, she heard mechanical, electrical sounds coming from behind a closed door.

The lights were dim throughout the house, almost as if no one was here (but who or what were the guards guarding, then?), and she crept slowly toward the closed door at the far end. Opening it gently, as silently as she could manage, Max stepped into a stripped-down bedroom illuminated only by the light coming from a TV on a raised table to her right. The volume was turned low, and the light changed as the picture did. In front of her was a single hospital bed surrounded by machines, each whirring as they fed oxygen and IV fluids to a dried-up prune of a man, on his back on the mattress.

The figure in the bed wasn't much bigger than Max had been when she'd fled Manticore. Stepping forward, she could see that the pruney lump was a very old gent with no hair, no teeth, and tiny black dots for eyes. Though the man's eyes were open, he seemed to see nothing, but his short, straight nose sniffed past the oxygen tube in his nostrils, as if he could smell her.

As she realized what she was seeing, Max felt the bottom drop out of her stomach and a chill sweep over her.

From behind her an icy male voice intoned, "Say hello to Lyman Cale, why don't you?"

Chapter Six
AS THE CROW FLIES

Max whirled to face a handsome blond man of about six feet and 180 pounds; he wore a black blazer over a white shirt with no tie, though his gray trousers had a disturbingly crisp crease for this time of night.

"Max . . . Guevera, isn't it?" he asked. His voice was a baritone that somehow managed to be both smooth and husky.

"Do I know you?" she asked, placing her hands on her hips, raising her chin, sending out confident body language that didn't truly reflect her current state of mind.

Even in the half-light provided by the television screen, the thirtyish man had piercing blue eyes—icy eyes; his pretty-boy looks were slightly undercut by a pug, piggish nose. His thin lips created a straight line that turned up maybe a tenth of an inch at each corner in what was, technically at least, a smile.

"We've not met," he admitted. "But I recognize you."

"From the TV," she said flatly.

"Yes . . . and I make it a business to know who's a friend of the Cale family, and who isn't."

"Then you know I'm a friend."

"A friend of Logan Cale's."

"Yes."

That assertion drew a leering appraisal, and the smile broadened into something uglier. "Logan always had an eye for the ladies."

"I am so flattered," she said dryly. "You know who I am. Be a good host—who the hell are you?"

He raised a scolding finger. "Be a good guest . . . I'm an old family friend—Franklin Bostock. Logan and I went to private school together, as boys. Ask him about me, sometime. I'd be amused to see if he recalls me fondly or not."

"I'll do that. Why is a family friend in Lyman Cale's bedroom at this hour?"

"A better question might be, why is a friend of Logan Cale's in Lyman Cale's bedroom at this hour? . . . My position right now is as Mr. Cale's private secretary."

Max gestured to the array of machines—one to help the patient breathe, a monitor that showed a stable heartbeat, reasonable blood pressure, and a barely perceptible nudge in the line that indicated brain activity. "What's wrong with Mr. Cale?"

Bostock made a clicking sound and shook his head. "I'm afraid Mr. Cale's had a series of debilitating strokes."

She frowned, wondering how Cale could have degenerated to this degree in so short a time. "Recently?"

"Fairly recently. He's been in a vegetative state for most of the last year and a half."

Eyes narrowing, she shook her head. "That's impossible. I just saw a video of him addressing Congress, what? Barely two months ago?"

The private secretary's smile returned, showing her another shade of self-satisfaction. "Video technology has come quite a long way, hasn't it? Feed some actual footage into CGI generating programs, and a person can live forever."

Max stepped near the bed, looked at the small pitiful form there, barely discernible as a human being. Quickly, she did the math on this situation, and strode over to Bostock, standing just a foot from him.

"Mr. Bostock, I came for Logan's uncle's help. But it looks like it's your help I need."

He bowed his head slightly. "As one family friend to another, I assure you I'll do what I can to be of assistance . . . Shall we go to my office?"

She followed Bostock out of the bedroom, leaving the frail old comatose figure to his unknowing privacy, and down the stairs to what must have been Lyman Cale's book-lined study until his private secretary had moved in and arrayed the massive mahogany desk with computer equipment. She was shown to a dark dimpled leather couch, and Bostock pulled a heavy chair around and sat, ready to listen attentively.

It took her less than five minutes to lay out the whole story for him. When she was finished, Bostock made that clicking sound again.

"I see," he sighed, shaking his head. "Obviously you believe Mr. Cale could put up that ransom."

She nodded slowly. "It would be a big help. It will probably be the thing that saves Logan's life, and I promise my first priority after recovering Mr. Cale's nephew will be to get that money back for you."

"From what I understand about your abilities," he said, "I believe you could return the ransom."

"Then . . . ?"

"I only wish we could provide it."

She gestured to the lavish surroundings. "Why can't you, Mr. Bostock?"

He arched an eyebrow, shrugged. "For the simple reason that we don't have the money. Or at least I can't access it."

She sat forward, almost climbing onto the man. "What's the problem here, Mr. Bostock? Surely you know that Logan is your employer's favorite nephew . . . and this is a family matter, an urgent, life-or-death—"

"Ms. Guevera—please. Your indignation is misplaced. Please keep in mind, I would have every right to call the police and have you taken out of here, bodily—for breaking and entering?"

Max did not back down. "What's going on in this house, Bostock? What the hell are you up to?"

"Nothing nefarious, I assure you. There is no money to access."

She pointed a finger ceilingward. "He may be in a coma, but Lyman Cale is wealthy as sin."

"He's sick as sin, too, Ms. Guevera. And his money is tied up in a conservatorship overseen by the trust department of the First National Bank of Seattle. The attorney in charge of the estate's fund would never agree to provide that ransom . . . and even if he did, I'm fairly certain the estate's full worth is well below your ransom figure of four million, at this point."

"But this mansion . . ."

"The mansion would find a fair price, even in today's market, yes. But do you really think a trust officer would allow this house to be quickly sold, or loaned against, to meet a kidnapper's demands?"

"Where's the money gone?"

"Being in a coma is an expensive hobby, Ms. Guevera—drugs, the nurses, the machines, the doctors, well . . . you get the drift."

"Dying costs as much as living."

His smile grew tight. "In Mr. Cale's case, much more."

Max could see that this guy was smooth and he was convincing, but bottom line? Bostock was nothing but a damned bureaucrat, and she could see that he wasn't going to try to help her. Her radar was tingling—she felt something was amiss here, and Bostock himself might well be behind it.

But she had no time to follow the trail of that instinct, not with the clock on Logan's life ticking . . .

And there was no talking to Lyman Cale. The uncle who would instantly have helped his beloved nephew had so many IVs and tubes running into him, no telling whether he was alive or dead . . .

A knock at the study door secured a "Come!" from Bostock, and two goons stepped in, both reacting to Max's black-clad presence with a lurch that Bostock froze with a raised hand.

"She's my guest," he told them.

These were the blond- and the brown-haired guards in TAC fatigues, the two who'd looked like pros. Closer up, they might have been twins; it was as if they'd been spawned from the same test tube, much like Max and her sibs. Both had Cro-Magnon foreheads, deep-set blue eyes, and tiny, nearly lipless mouths. What neither of them had was anything resembling a neck, their skulls seeming to simply swivel atop their shoulders, their attention on her even as they listened to Bostock.

"However," their superior was saying, "I think Ms. Guevera's visit is at an end, since I don't see any way of helping her at the moment."

She said nothing—just looked hard at him, letting the private secretary know she sensed something was *not* right.

All this inspired in Bostock was another smile—he had displayed perhaps a dozen variations, all of which she was learning to despise. "Otto? Franz? Would you escort Ms. Guevera off the property, please? . . . I'm sure she'll be glad to show you where she left her means of transportation."

The two goons followed her all the way down to where she'd beached the raft. She dragged the raft to the edge of the water, then glanced up at them. "How long has the old man been sick?"

No reaction—the heads didn't even swivel on the no-necks.

"What's Bostock like to work for?"

No response. They just looked at her like two more Dobermans contemplating an attack; and her all out of hamburger . . .

"You two just don't have any lines in this little melodrama, do you?"

Contradicting her, Otto (or was it Franz?) said, "Just get the hell out of here."

"You made us look stupid," Franz said (or was it Otto?).

"I had help," she said, and eased the raft in.

She rolled in over the side and picked up her oar. She slid the oar into the water and gently turned the raft toward Puget Sound proper and the speedboat that waited for her a mile out.

As she rowed into the darkness, Otto (Franz?) yelled, "Next time *you'll* look stupid!"

Thinking that Franz (Otto?) might well be right, Max kept rowing. The darkness out here was complete. The moon hid behind a cloud and the stars seemed to have run for cover as well.

Her spirits were low, as the thought occurred to her that she might have seen Logan for the last time. Twenty-four hours ago she'd never wanted to see him again, and was willing for the last words he ever heard from her to be words of anger, even hatred.

And at that moment, she *had* hated him. Or thought she did.

Logan, of all people, knew that everyone she had ever known had lied to her from the day she was born. He was supposed to be different, better than the rest of the world. But was that fair? Or even possible? Did Logan have to be perfect?

She shook her head as she rowed, getting angry all over again. Not perfect, she thought, just honest.

The waters remained as smooth as the emotional

whirlpool within her was not. From a flash of yesterday's anger to the overwhelming desire to see Logan again, to hold him, to forgive him, to give him a new start to make new promises that he damn well better—

She shivered at her own inner turmoil. As she stroked with the oar, she listened to the gentle lapping and she forced the emotions down. She had been trained to be a soldier, and goddamnit, she would be a solider.

She would fight for the man she loved.

And God help anyone who had hurt him, and if someone had killed Logan, that person would be beyond even God's help . . . because she would bring hell down on the killer.

Looking uncharacteristically disheveled, Alec sat in the Terminal City control room while Luke hovered over him like an onion-headed mother hen. The core crew of transgenics worked the monitors—Mole (absent momentarily on a bathroom break), Luke, and Dix, the latter occupying his commander's chair. Right now, however, Luke was stitching up a wound in Alec's hand.

"You're exaggerating," Luke said, but there was awe in his voice.

"No, I'm tellin' ya," Alec said. "That tree was five feet from the roof, and twenty feet down." And he wasn't overselling the length of his jump from the roof of the Volunteer Park water tower, either. He'd had plenty of time to gain velocity as the tree rushed up to meet him.

"I thought pine was supposed to be a soft wood," Alec said. "Well, I'm exhibit A—that theory's BS. Owww!"

"Sorry," Luke said.

Luke had already wrapped two cracked ribs, applied some smelly homemade salve on half a dozen bruises, and stitched up a cut on Alec's arm. The black eye, he'd told Alec, would have to heal on its own.

"They used to put a piece of raw steak on 'em," Alec said, gesturing to the shiner.

From his high command seat, Dix growled, "I'll get right on that."

Despite his sprained ankle, Alec had managed to make it back to his motorcycle before Badar Tremaine's orders for his boys to search the woods had gotten under way.

"I'll wrap the ankle next," Luke said, "then we're done."

Mole strode in then and looked Alec over from top to bottom. "You look like shit," he announced.

"So do you, buddy, but I'm gonna heal."

Grinning as he chomped on his cigar, Mole bumped fists with Alec. "Glad that five-hundred-foot fall didn't break your funny bone."

"Broke pretty much everything else, though."

Mole pulled up a kitchen chair; the seats were salvaged from here and there, this and that—Alec was in a frayed stuffing-spouting easy chair, and Luke was up and down out of an office swivel job.

"What," Mole asked, "are we going to do if Max comes back without the money?"

Alec shared what he'd overheard at the tower.

Then Mole said, "Any suggestions?"

"We know where the money drop is—why don't just get there first?"

The ransom note, delivered to Logan's apartment, said the drop would be at sunup at Gas Works Park, near the old plant.

Completing Alec's thread, Mole said, "And hit 'em when they show up?"

Nodding, Alec said, "What better time? Hit 'em before they even get set up. You know damn well they're planning some sort of trap or double cross."

The lizard face wrinkled further. "We do?"

"I been thinking—this could be about Max."

"Max. But it's Logan they kidnapped."

"Right, Mole . . . and they left a ransom note at Logan's apartment. And who was that ransom note intended for?"

Mole shrugged. "Those dipshits didn't 'intend' it for anybody special—they just knew Logan was a rich guy and figured his rich family would pay the ticket, or his people, or . . . whoever."

"It was *addressed* to Max."

"A four-million-dollar ransom note . . . addressed to Max. Alec, look at where you are—who sends a ransom note to Terminal City, expecting four million bucks to be layin' around?"

"My point exactly. More precisely, who knows about Logan's apartment?"

"Nobody," Mole shrugged.

"*Somebody* knows about it—or otherwise a bunch

of nobodies called the Furies wouldn'ta snatched Logan."

Mole's cigar traveled from the corner of one side of his mouth to the other one. "So . . . what does it mean?"

Alec shrugged. "I'm smart enough to come up with the questions. I was hoping somebody else'd be smart enough to come up with the answers . . . They called Logan 'the troll' . . . What could that be about?"

"The troll," Mole said. "You're sure they called him that?"

"Well . . . no. I'm not sure what the hell they meant."

"Could be a place."

Alec made a face. "A place called the Troll?"

"The Fremont Troll?" Mole offered.

Alec shook his head. "No clue. Try English."

Mole shook his head. "You don't know about the Fremont Troll? How long have you lived in Seattle, man?"

"Fremont Troll," Alec echoed.

"Yeah. You know the Aurora Avenue bridge?"

"Been over it a few times."

"Ever been under it?"

Alec gave him a look. "Maybe that's where you take *your* dates, but I'm a little classier kind of guy."

"No, shit-for-brains," Mole said, and the cigar butt traveled again, "it's this giant sculpture under the bridge. Looks like a big bearded dude on his belly."

"What have you been smoking?"

"He's got this car in one hand, like a bug he snatched up."

"What have you been drinking?"

"Thing is freakin' huge, man. I can't believe you've never seen it."

"A bearded guy with a car in his hand? You expect me to buy that."

Mole slapped himself on the forehead and uttered a string of four letter words, in the process chewing the end of his cigar to pulp.

"What idiot thing did he say now?" Max asked, striding into the center and looking down at the seated Alec, still being mothered by Luke.

"Dude never heard of the Fremont Troll," Mole said, trying to relight what was left of the butt.

Max looked at Alec's pitiful-looking black eye and said, "No way."

"I'll believe it when I see it," Alec said. "You're all just jerkin' my chain."

Crossing her arms, Max eyed the handsome, bandaged-up X5 suspiciously. "And who did *you* lose a fight with?"

"A tree," was all he said. "How did it go with Logan's uncle?"

She told them. "Any ideas?"

Alec filled her in about his expedition, and he and Mole described their plan for a two-pronged invasion before the scheduled sunup drop-off of the "supposed" ransom—one team going to Gas Works Park, the other to the under-the-bridge troll statue.

"It's a plan," Max said, nodding.

The Furies were a large, powerful gang, but they were ordinaries, which meant that Max and her crew of transgenics had a big advantage. What the Terminal

City team lacked in numbers, they made up for in genetics and training.

"I don't want Clemente down on us for this," Max said, referring to Detective Ramon Clemente, the Seattle cop who had collaborated with her to keep both the Jam Pony hostage crisis and the siege at Terminal City from turning into bloodbaths.

"Don't give it a thought," Alec said. "We'll be in and out before the cops even know what happened."

Mole nodded. "They won't know what hit them."

"Two groups, then," Max said.

Another nod from Mole. "I'll go with Alec—you round up Joshua."

"All right," she said. "In one hour, we're in position."

"Better make it an hour and a half," Alec said. "Luke hasn't finished taping up my ankle yet."

Mole glowered at him. "Pass for an ordinary long enough, you get to be a wuss like one."

Alec gave him a sarcastically beaming look. "And yet still you choose me to team up with."

Starting up a new stogie, the lizard man said, "Somebody's got to keep you from getting your ass beat by another tree."

Max raised her hands, palms out, calling a halt to the floor show. "An hour and a half it is," she said. "Be ready, and don't tell anybody. The quieter we keep this, the better off we'll all be."

Alec said, "You don't know how right you are."

She frowned at him. "Meaning?"

"Somebody had to tip the Furies off about where

Logan lived, right? And who knows that besides our fellow Terminal City residents?"

Mole said, "That cop Clemente—a few others that were around the night Kelpy bought it."

"Wait, wait, wait," Max said. "Are you suggesting we have a traitor in our midst?"

"I'm suggesting just what I suggested: somebody tipped the Furies off about Logan's private pad. I mean, you didn't tell 'em, did you, Max?"

"No, Alec. It would have to be somebody terminally untrustworthy—anybody come to mind?"

His eyes widened. "Hey—I don't deserve that."

Max's expression softened. "Actually, you don't. And you raise a good point—someone tipped the Furies about Logan. But we don't have time to find out who. Saving Logan's ass is our top, our only, priority."

Alec nodded. So did Mole, and Dix in his command chair, even though he wasn't supposed to be listening in, and Luke as he taped the bandage around Alec's ankle.

"What we're up to," Max said again, "stays among us, and Joshua—just the core group . . . Now, let's jet."

Ninety minutes later Alec finally met the Fremont Troll.

Under the north end of the Aurora Avenue bridge, the reclining stone troll rose eighteen feet, nearly bumping its head on the underside of the bridge. The troll looked just as Mole had described him—longhaired with one shiny metal eye, crawling on its belly, the fingers of his right hand spread, its left fist closed around a gray hulk of a car.

Alec and Mole climbed up behind the troll peeking out from the darkness under the bridge. Rolling his head on the column of his neck to ease the stiffness, Alec settled in for a wait.

No telling how long it would take the Furies to get there with Logan, but a glance at his watch told him it could be up to two hours till the scheduled hostage/ransom exchange.

"Mole," he said. "I'm beat."

"Sleep, then," he said. "I got it covered."

"I'm just gonna shut my eyes. Rest a little."

"Go ahead."

When his phone trilled and he bolted upright, Alec had no idea how long he'd been out. The tiny ring echoed like a church bell beneath the bridge.

"You answer it," Mole growled, "or I break it." The lizard man still had a lit cigar clamped between his teeth and had apparently managed to stay awake through Alec's nap.

Quickly, Alec fished the phone out of his pocket and punched the button on the start of the second ring. "What?" he asked.

"Anything?"

Max's hushed voice. She'd be at Gas Works Park, with the others.

"No," he said, but looked to Mole for confirmation. With a derisive snort, the lizard man nodded—nothing had happened. "How about you?"

"Nobody," she said. "And they're overdue."

"Well, they'd stop here first, surely—to deposit their hostage."

"You'd think. But Joshua's stood ground while I've roved the area—nobody sniffin', nothing."

"What's your read, Max?"

"Either something's gone wrong, or the Furies are playing some new game."

"Hate when that happens . . . Maybe they're just waiting for you to leave."

"Nope," she said. "I got an A-plus in recon. Trust me, they're not here. And that bag's just sittin' there—even the bugs aren't goin' near it."

"Not good, Max."

"Almost two hours after sunup and nothing—something has definitely gone wrong."

The bag she referred to was a leather valise they had packed with a cake of bricks and newspaper, under a frosting of smaller bills. If anybody picked the thing up, it'd weigh enough to pass for four million dollars, and a casual opening would reveal money on top. Only a more aggressive search would reveal the ploy.

But from what Max was saying, no one seemed interested enough to even look and see if they were being ripped off.

"We need to make a move," Alec said, surprised that Mole had let him sleep this long without kicking him. "Agreed?"

"Agreed."

"Any ideas, Max?"

". . . I think we should visit the Furies' home."

"The four of us . . . just drop by?"

"That's the plan, Alec."

"And you say *my* plans suck."

"You up for it?"

"Yeah. No problem."

"Sit tight. Fill Mole in, and Joshua and me, we'll be right over—then we'll blaze."

Gunning her Ninja, Max flew through the open gate of Lakeview Cemetery, Joshua clinging on behind her, hanging on with just his left hand, the valise full of bricks, newspapers, and a few dollars swinging from his right hand.

On Alec's motorcycle, the handsome X5 and a lizard-faced passenger were trailing a bike length behind. The engines roared throatily as they cut across the lawn away from the paved road. Though the road sliced through the cemetery and ended near the Furies' HQ, Max didn't want to take the direct approach. The Furies would have numbers, so that meant it was important that the transgenics have surprise on their side.

Immediately, as arranged, the speed on both bikes was cut and their engine roar settled into a humming purr.

Max made a quick hand signal and Alec peeled off to the right, his bike gliding across the grass, in and around gravestones, Mole looking vaguely disgusted having to hang onto the X5. Max and Joshua took off to the left, also keeping the speed and engine sound minimal. The idea was to come at the Furies' HQ from two sides.

The HQ had at one time been a mausoleum constructed after the Pulse, not far from the graves of Bruce and Brandon Lee. Max had actually visited the graves before, not long after she'd come to Seattle. The graves had reminded her of the old days, back at Mann's Chinese Theater in Los Angeles, living with the Clan, with her mentor Moody and the young man named Fresca. Back then, Moody would run movies in the theater from time to time. One had been this really cool kung fu flick called *Enter the Dragon*, and had starred Bruce Lee.

She had seen the late kung fu star's son Brandon in a movie called *The Crow*, but that had been on a cheesy video player with a bad tape. Before the Furies took over, the mausoleum HQ had been that of an Asian street gang called the Crows, so-called in honor of the late Brandon; but Badar Tremaine's forces had wiped them out, six or seven years ago.

The mausoleum stood maybe fifteen feet tall and was at least twenty-five yards long and almost as wide—suitable to house the remains of a small town.

And even that had not been big enough for the Furies, the cement wall at one end serving as a brace for a lean-to extension that had been cobbled on. The doors at either end were wooden now, the weathered coffins that had formerly been stored inside now stacked outside like so much cord wood.

Within seconds of each other the two motorcycles arrived on either side of the mausoleum. Max kicked her cycle to loud, throbbing life and Alec followed suit. Their timing synchronized, the two motorcycles broke down the doors at either end of the mausoleum as they crashed splinteringly through.

Barely inside, both Max and Alec braked, burning rubber, screeching to a halt; they laid their bikes down, the four of them rolling off and coming up in combat stances, ready for action, expecting anything . . .

Just about anything.

They froze.

All around them, Furies lay dead.

Blood painted the walls in vivid splashes, recent enough to still be a dripping red; the floor, the meager furnishings, dribbled gore. Tables and chairs were overturned, TVs smashed, and a long wood bar that ran along one wall was pocked with bullet marks.

Max and her transgenic brothers had come prepared for a fight; what they found instead was a massacre.

Bodies lay everywhere, sprawled in various postures of surprised violent death—shot, stabbed, slashed. Whoever or whatever had done this had accomplished it with great speed and no mercy. Easily a hundred of the Furies, probably every member, had been slaughtered, and from the looks of things, they hadn't had time to put up much of a fight.

This was not the aftermath of a battle. Some spent cartridges lay scattered around, but any sign of casualties the Furies might have inflicted on their opponents were gone, if there ever had been any.

"God," Mole said.

"Damn," Alec said.

"Logan," Max said, the word spoken with the reverence of a prayer, edged with the sort of sorrow that had been present so often at graveside services nearby.

Without being told, Alec and Mole went back to the doors on either end, standing guard in case whoever committed this carnage was nearby or planned a return. Max and Joshua crept through the roomful of bodies, walking gingerly, as if to not wake them, and searched for Logan.

Max recognized members of the kidnap team among the corpses. The night of Logan's kidnapping, they had presented little trouble to her, until the Tazer came out of nowhere; but whoever did this was working with heavier artillery. It was plain to see that not only had the bangers been shot to death, someone had obviously walked along strafing the bodies with automatic weapons fire, just making sure. Others had been sliced and diced—machetes, she thought—like so much meat being prepared for a giant cannibal's stew.

Amid all of this Max walked, terrified that she would find Logan among the dead . . .

. . . though if she found him, at least, she would *know*. How terrible not to find him, and never to know what happened to him . . .

From the other side of the room, Joshua said, "Logan not here, Little Fella."

Though he kept his voice low, it boomed off the mausoleum walls and seemed to echo in her skull. She thought that gunfire in here, this much gunfire, would have sounded like the end of the world—reports rocketing around the walls, bouncing this way and that.

"Sad," Joshua was saying. "So sad."

They had come to fight these Furies, to kill if necessary; but to see this massacre was to pity the victims in death, whoever, whatever, they might have been in life.

Her half of the room revealed no sign of Logan either, but there was the cutout in the far wall that led to the wooden add-on they had seen from the outside. As she approached the shadowy hole, Max's heart pounded and she wondered if the others could hear it, echoing off the blood-spattered walls. Beads of sweat pearled her forehead, even though it was still cold both outside and in this unheated mausoleum.

There was light beyond the opening, but she couldn't make anything out yet, and no one had called out to them; of course, Logan might have been tied up, and gagged . . . But if so, the marauders who'd committed this atrocity would hardly have spared him.

Still, this was the last possible place—if Logan was here, he would be in that add-on room. Willing herself to move forward, she took a few steps, her feet feeling impossibly heavy, as if she were turning into a stone gargoyle to adorn this cemetery.

And as she slipped through the hole cut in the wall, she could see one person sitting at a table, a man, his back to her.

She felt a snake of revulsion slither in her gut as she realized that the body was headless.

The room was small, barely ten feet across, with a square table in the center, one wooden chair drawn up to it, holding the seated body—not Logan, apparently, as the corpse wore the black T-shirt and jeans of a Fury—three matching chairs scattered on the floor. In the corner, a small TV had been smashed.

Moving forward, she looked over the shoulder of the body at the table and saw what was presumably the body's former head on a plate in front of it, the face recognizable as that of Badar Tremaine, leader of the Furies.

Despite herself, she let out a sigh of relief as she confirmed that Logan was nowhere in the room. If he wasn't here, he might still be alive somewhere.

Taking another look at Tremaine's head on the plate, she noticed an object sticking out from his mouth. Though not squeamish, Max shivered, and buried the impulse to turn and flee, instead going over to the detached head for a closer look at the protruding object.

Whatever it was, it was metallic and not very large, the cylindrical end sticking out like a stiff, silver tongue.

Slowly, as the gang leader's dead eyes stared at her, she withdrew the metal object from the slack mouth . . .

. . . a minicassette recorder.

The other three entered the small room, Mole first, saying, "Doesn't look like anyone's coming back. When you already killed everything that moves, a return trip's kinda pointless."

"Fubar," Joshua breathed, looking at the body.

It was a word Alec had taught him and Max didn't care for.

Alec was at Max's side. He said, "Badar Tremaine—well, he *was* the head man."

Max shot him a glare.

"Sorry," he said. "Couldn't help myself . . . I mean, he is sitting at the head of the table."

Joshua grabbed Alec's arm. "No jokes. That headless man . . . what if it was Logan?"

"But it isn't," Alec said, glancing over at the object in Max's hand. "What have you got there?"

On Badar's T-shirt, she wiped saliva and blood from the little machine. "Tape recorder."

"Press 'play' yet?"

Alec, Joshua, and Mole were gathered around her, near the table with their headless host. She looked from face to face among her three friends.

"Go on," Mole said. "Maybe it's a message."

She let out some air, and pushed the Play button.

"Hello, 452."

They all recognized the voice instantly.

"I knew," Ames White's vaguely processed voice said from the tiny machine in her palm, *"you would never just deliver the ransom and pay to get your friend back. You're not built like that. You can never play by the rules, can you, 452? I can relate."*

The urge to throw the recorder off the wall was nearly overwhelming.

"That's why I employed the Furies, to acquire my hostage. I knew you would track them down. And, of course, they couldn't be left alive to talk to anyone about certain arrangements I made with them . . . So as you can see, I made new *arrangements with them, this evening."*

She glanced down at the unseeing eyes of Badar Tremaine.

"The media might even get the story that vengeful transgenics killed the whole gang. I'm fairly sure some good citizen will pass that information along. After all, the raid on Logan Cale's apartment was close to Terminal City, and the victim was . . . is . . . a friend of yours."

Joshua growled low and deep in the back of his throat.

"Now that we know the lengths you'll go to in order to get your friend back—and now that your friend is in my personal custody—it's important that we talk about the real ransom."

"Bastard's been playin' us since jump," Alec said.

"You know what I want, 452. Think."

As if answering the voice, Max shook her head. This had gone from bad to much, much worse . . .

"This is your karma . . . You New Age Terminal City trolls believe in that nonsense, right? You see, you took my son from me. So I took Logan Cale from you."

"Damnit," Max said, her voice hard and cold.

"You want your friend back," White's voice said. *"Well, I want Ray back . . . Getting the idea?"*

"Yes, you son of a bitch," she said. "Yes."

"Stay by your cell phone, 452. I'll be in touch. You have three days to comply, or your friend dies. Oh, and, uh . . . Merry Christmas."

Chapter Seven

DEATH RAY

A woman named Wendy Olsen had been looking for her son.

The boy had been kidnapped, and Mrs. Olsen came to Eyes Only for help in finding—and retrieving—young Ray. Logan's investigation was already under way when he brought Max aboard, sharing with her the shocking revelation that the boy they were looking for was the son of NSA agent Ames White.

For several years various Seattle citizens—disenfranchised from city, state, and federal governments that seemed on the one hand uncaring and on the other corrupt—had turned to Eyes Only, seeking underground aid in situations like these. Logan would do his utmost to resolve such problems, utilizing his operatives, and for almost two years Max had been his chief field agent.

And Max and Logan had indeed—true to form—rescued the boy, Ray, carrying the child away from Brookridge Academy, a private school that served as a front for the cult Ames White served, the so-called "Familiars."

Ray had been weak—the result of a typically twisted snake cult ritual that involved slicing the boy's arm with a sword dipped in venomous blood— but White's son had somehow survived the attentions of the Familiars. Unfortunately, the same could not be said for his mother.

When she went to the town of Willoughby, in search of her missing son, Wendy Olsen White was murdered . . . by her own husband.

In the end, Logan had located Wendy's sister, and Ray had been sent to live with her. Logan—using his seemingly endless string of Eyes Only operatives, a modern day underground railroad—had helped the pair vanish, their whereabouts unknown even to Max.

Now the only option open to Max was to play White's game—to retrieve and deliver his son to him; and walk right into a trap. There'd be no fooling Ames White; she might have duped the Furies, but White and his snake cult associates—demented and deluded though they might be—were as shrewd as they were smart.

And she knew they were as vicious as they were smart—just ask the Furies . . . try using a Ouija board . . .

She knew damn well there would be no hostage-for-hostage trade: end game for the snake cult would include her death. That much had been made clear to Max in her previous encounters with the bizarre cult.

Still, she figured they would have to do whatever White asked; her only hope to save Logan—and herself, and the lives of those helping her, and the boy Ray, for that matter—would be to walk into the lion's den and beard the bastards.

The problem was, she wasn't sure how to accomplish the vital first step—finding the boy Logan had so skillfully hidden away, a step that Ames White no doubt assumed she would be able to accomplish easily. Without Logan to help her, Max's efforts would be blocked by Eyes Only's own security measures, designed to protect the boy from White and the Familiars.

In the kidnappings she and Logan had thwarted together, Logan found the clues, and Max grabbed up the missing person—that was the program, that was how it had always gone down.

Now, with Logan MIA—in fact, with Logan one of two key MIAs—she was left to her own devices to locate the other missing person, Ray, and secure him . . .

And it wasn't like Ray was a normal missing person. Logan—a master at concealing people, at giving them new starts—had made the boy disappear, so that he would never be found even by his own father and White's formidable network of NSA and snake cult allies. She'd be finding a needle in a haystack—only she didn't even know where the damn haystack was.

They left the carnage of the cemetery behind—should the cops show, they didn't want to seed the press for another transgenics media storm—and repaired to a small café. Nestled in a back booth, over the warmth of hot steaming cups of coffee, the four comrades sat—Joshua, Alec, and Mole watching her, waiting for her decision.

She was their leader, and they would follow her through the gates of Hell, if necessary; she knew as much, and she appreciated it . . . and this time, the gates of Hell were exactly where she'd be taking them.

On her cell phone, Max called Dix and quickly laid out the situation.

"Who do you want me to kill?" Dix asked.

"We'll get to that," she said. "Right now, it's your brain I need."

"Good. I just hate it when women want me for my good looks."

"Bet you do. I need you and Luke to take a crack at decrypting Logan's hard drive."

"Ouch. Couldn't we just crack the Pentagon data banks, or somethin' easy? Frickin' Logan, he's the best, y'know."

"I know. But Logan says you and Luke are the best hackers he ever ran into."

"No shit?"

"None at all," she said, lying through her teeth. "Get on it."

"All over it," Dix promised; but uncertainty peeked out around the edges of his bravado.

She clicked off and looked at her three friends, Joshua next to her in the booth, Alec and Mole across. "Logan hid this kid away so that God couldn't find him. But we have to."

"What?" Alec said, frowning. "And turn him over to White?"

Shifting his dead cigar from one side of his mouth

to the other, leaning forward, Mole said, "Max—you know I will follow your lead."

"I appreciate that."

"But this—big mistake."

"Why?" she asked, and she couldn't keep the defensive edge out of her tone.

Mole relighted that stogie; got it going good; then he gazed at her, hard. "Why did Logan hide that kid away? To keep him away from daddy dearest. Now we're going to do White's damn dirty work for him? Tell me there's another way."

"Is there another way?"

All three just looked at her.

Finally Alec said, "You figure we go through with the exchange and, what? Just vamp? Improvise our way out of it, shooting up as many snake-cult goofballs as we can? And hope for the best? . . . Again, I have to say it: and you think *my* plans suck?"

Max said, "What . . . other . . . choice . . . do . . . we . . . *have*?"

"You know what choice we have," Mole said.

Max said nothing.

"He takes one for the team," Mole said.

"Logan?" She practically shrieked this response, and hated herself for the "girl" softness of that.

Alec shook his head, but he was agreeing with Mole as he said, "Man knew the risks of gettin' involved with Eyes Only—that's how he ended up in the wheelchair in the first place."

Sitting forward, Max said, "No one knows that better than—"

"You're a solider, Max," Mole cut in. "We all

are . . . And so, in his way, is Logan. Do you *really*
think Logan would want you to turn the kid over to
White, just like that? After you risked so much res-
cuin' the brat? After he put so much effort in saltin'
the kid away? No. No way."

Max turned to Joshua, whose lionlike features were
draped with sorrow. "What do you think, Big Fella?"

Joshua covered his face with a pawlike hand. He
was crying.

Max touched his arm. "Joshua . . ."

"Logan," Joshua said. "Have to respect . . . what
Logan would want." He lowered his hand and gazed
at her, his hairy face matted with tears. "Mole is right.
Logan. Take one. For the team."

Even Joshua could see it—and now so could she.
Everything they were saying was true. But that did
not mean she would roll over and allow Logan to die
at the hands of Ames White—not while there was
breath in her body.

"You're right," she said, "and you're wrong."

Alec arched an eyebrow.

Mole rolled his stogie around.

Joshua dried his eyes with a napkin.

"You're right that we can't just turn Ray over
to White," she said. "That would negate everything
Logan stands for—everything we've stood for . . .
But we don't walk away from a brother. We don't sac-
rifice any one of us unless we absolutely have to."

Alec said, "I'm sensing a Plan B."

She nodded. "We still need to find Ray White. We
still need that boy."

Alec frowned. "We find him . . . blow his cover . . .

yank the kid out of hiding . . . and then we *don't* turn him over . . . ?"

"That's right—and, Alec, my plan doesn't suck."

"Of what use is Ray White to us," Alec said, "if we don't turn him over?"

But Mole was ahead of the X5, eyes tight in the lizard face. "Bait."

Max smiled and nodded. "Got it in one, Mole."

But Alec and Joshua weren't on the same page, the former shaking his head, the other squinting in confusion.

Max pressed on: "Ames White is going to insist on talking to Ray at some point."

"A given," said Mole.

"Well, if we've got the kid, even for White just to talk to on the phone, if he knows we *really* have the boy, we've got a chance of getting Logan back. Or do you really wanna walk away and let Logan Cale 'take one for the team'?"

Alec, typically, just cocked his head like a beagle who wasn't sure he'd understood the question.

"We gotta try," Mole said. "He'd do the same for us."

"How about you, Alec?" Max asked.

"What?"

"Do we walk away?"

"No."

"No?"

"I mean . . . hell, no."

The self-absorbed X5 still didn't seem to be fully on board, but at least he wasn't fighting her anymore.

Mole said, "Max, one thing is understood . . . we

don't give the kid up to White under any circumstances."

She'd lost her head for a while, allowing her feelings for Logan to cloud the bigger picture. Now her friends had her back on track. They would use Ray to draw White out, but that was all.

She said, "No way White gets the boy. No way in hell."

Alec lifted his coffee cup. "I'm in," he said, and they toasted—Joshua hitting the cups a little too hard, spilling some coffee.

A lot more than coffee would be spilled in the days ahead.

"Here's where we are," Max said. "Dix and Luke are trying to crack Logan's computer, but I doubt they'll have much if any luck. White and his NSA goon squad took the old one, when they raided Logan's prior apartment, and they *still* haven't cracked the codes."

"You know that for sure?" Alec asked.

She nodded. "Comes straight from Otto Gottlieb."

Gottlieb, White's former partner in the NSA, had seen the light and helped the transgenics capture Kelpy and bring White down at the NSA. Max wondered if Gottlieb could be of any help on this outing.

But Gottlieb had been rewarded by the NSA with a raise and promotion, for his whistle-blowing on White, and Max was afraid his loyalties these days might be too strongly NSA for her to risk trusting his involvement.

Alec said, "Why don't I talk to Matt Sung—he might be able to help."

Matt Sung, an Asian-American detective for the Seattle P.D., had helped Eyes Only on numerous occasions.

"Good call," Max said. "Logan trusts Matt completely." Then, turning to Mole, she added, "Can you track down Bling?"

Mole's cigar bobbed as he nodded. "Count on it."

Bling—Logan's African-American physical therapist and occasional driver/bodyguard—knew more about Eyes Only operations than anybody this side of Logan himself.

With Logan wearing the exoskeleton more and more, Bling found himself with free time, now that Logan was doing less rehab and getting himself around. They hadn't seen Bling for several months, but she knew Logan talked to him regularly and was sure he was still in the city somewhere.

"How can Joshua help?" Joshua asked.

Max couldn't exactly send a six-foot-four-inch Dog Boy out to do anything inconspicuous; when it came time to kick ass and take names, Joshua would be the point man. But she couldn't bench him now—it would hurt Joshua, whose fondness for Logan she found touching.

She said, "Go over to Father's house and look around. Logan laid low there for a while—maybe he left something behind that'll lead us to the boy."

Father's house had once belonged to Sandeman, the enigmatic and benign figure behind the transgenics program that Manticore had corrupted; Joshua had lived there for a while, and Logan had been a frequent visitor who'd often crashed there, after his apartment was trashed by White and the NSA.

Joshua nodded eagerly, happy to be part of the effort.

"What about you?" Alec asked.

"I've got a plan of my own," she said.

Alec gave her a wicked little smile. "Hope it doesn't suck."

She traded him smirk for smirk. "Me, too . . . We'll meet back at Terminal City in two hours. Use the cell phones to keep in touch—if you find something, don't save it up for later. Call me *right now.*"

They all nodded.

She let out a huge sigh and slid off the booth. Outside on the street, she said, "Okay—let's go find that kid."

"Why don't we?" Alec said. His black eye had healed already—those good transgenic genes.

Fists were bumped, and they went their separate ways. Joshua—understandably shy about being seen in public—opted to return to his old house via the sewer system. Max would pit Joshua's knowledge of the sewer system against anyone's, even the engineers who designed it. When it came to underground travel, Joshua was king.

It was agreed that Mole would drop Alec at Matt Sung's precinct, after which Mole would continue on with the X5's cycle in search of Bling. For her part, Max was off to some old stomping grounds.

Might have been yesterday that she last leaned on the bar in Crash; but in reality, she hadn't set foot in the place in six months, not since that day everything went sideways at Jam Pony.

The converted warehouse was separated into three rooms by its rounded brick archways. Video monitors attached to the walls and the big screen TV in the middle room all still showed footage of violent collisions between cars, trains, buses, motorcycles, anything mechanical, providing the crashes that were the bar's namesake. Manhole cover tables were scattered around, each surrounded by four or five chairs. The far room held pool and foosball tables. The entire wall behind the bar was a backlit Plexiglas sculpture constructed of bicycle frames.

Max sat at the bar nursing a diet cola. The scene at the Furies' mausoleum had put her in the mood for something harder, but she needed to keep her wits about her. For now, all she could do was cool her jets and hope she wouldn't have to wait too long.

She didn't.

In less than ten minutes a woman opened the door and stood in silhouette against the bright sunshine. The door closed slowly and Max's eyes readjusted to the dim light as the woman came down the stairs, spotted Max, and came over to take a seat next to her at the bar.

A slim blonde with her short hair tucked neatly up under a stocking cap, the woman was mannequin thin with alabaster skin, standing slightly taller than Max, with large dark eyes. When the blonde sat down, Max got a glimpse of the tattoo on the woman's back, just about waist level.

"Asha," Max said, by way of hello.

The blonde's smile showed some teeth, but seemed forced. She and Max had never been friends, exactly, even if they had been allies much of the time. Max knew Asha had a thing for Logan, and she wouldn't have been at all surprised if the blonde still resented Logan picking her.

"Max," Asha said, with a curt nod.

That was the extent of their chitchat.

After Asha ordered a coffee for herself, Max laid out the situation—Asha's only reaction to hearing of Logan's kidnapping was a tightening between her eyebrows, but that spoke volumes—then Max told Asha what she needed.

Asha's eyes tightened, and her mouth did, too. "You really think I'm gonna betray Logan's trust?"

Max shrugged. "Only if you want to save his life."

The blonde took a sip of her coffee and carefully set the cup on the bar in front of her. Her eyes never left the cup as she said nothing for a very long minute.

Then her eyes rose and she said, quietly, "If I tell you anything, Logan will never speak to me again."

"If he's dead," Max pointed out, "he'll never speak to anyone again."

She shook her head, and the blonde hair shimmered with barroom neon. "He'll never be able to trust me."

Max let out a breath. "Asha, he'll never know I got it from you. You have my word."

Asha studied Max for a good thirty seconds—it seemed an endless time to Max, but she let the blonde make up her own mind.

Finally Asha spoke. "I believe you, I really do.

Despite our . . . differences, you've been honest with me. And I would help you if I could."

"But?"

"I really don't think I know anything."

"Sounds to me like you're not sure . . . Any little thing you could share would be more than I have right now."

Again Asha shook her head. "You're asking me to betray a trust. Do you know what it does, between two people, when trust is shattered? When one betrays the other?"

Max looked away.

"What?" Asha said.

"Nothing." Max shook her head, smiled a bitter little smile, and said, "We don't have the luxury of social niceties right now, Asha. I'm afraid 'betraying' Logan's trust is the only way of saving Logan's *life*."

Looking back into her coffee, Asha kept her voice low, barely above a whisper. "All right . . . all right. But I don't remember the woman's name—the aunt?"

Max nodded slightly, one eye going to the bartender to make sure he wasn't watching them.

"And I didn't have all that much to do with it," Asha continued. "I tracked the woman down, introduced her to Logan. The rest was Eyes Only."

Like most of Logan's operatives, Asha did not know that Logan *was* Eyes Only.

"I understand," Max said.

"All I can tell you is, the aunt lived in Fremont. Once Logan reunited her with her nephew, he gave her the money and the new papers to make the move. I did hear him mention Appleton."

"Appleton . . . about an hour and a half from here? Upstate?"

"I don't know. Could be some other Appleton in Arkansas or Maine, who the hell knows. Would Logan salt somebody away so close to home?"

"Actually, he might. It's unexpected enough . . . Asha, *think*—"

She shook her head, hair shimmering with neon again. "Max, honestly—that's all I know. Really."

"Thanks, Asha." And she touched the woman's hand on the bar. "I appreciate it."

Asha gripped Max's hand; the squeeze they exchanged was the most personal, warmest moment they'd ever shared. "You save his fine ass, girl—understood?"

"Understood."

"And you didn't hear any of this from me."

"Also understood."

Appleton.

It wasn't much.

But it was more than she had when she came in to Crash, wasn't it? Tossing some money on the bar, Max retreated up the stairs and out into the bright sunlit day. As she rode back to Terminal City on her Ninja, she wondered if the others were having any luck. Her pickings were pretty damn slim.

Alec was already there, in the control room, when Max strode in.

"How'd you do?" she asked.

He shook his head. "Zip, zally, zero. Sung didn't sing—he doesn't know anything about the White kid."

"*Says* he doesn't know, or doesn't know?"

"I didn't hook him up to a lie detector, Max, but I know a lot about lying . . . and I don't think he was. Besides, you know how highly Logan regards Sung."

She wondered if Alec had run into another Eyes Only loyalist who was refusing to share info out of respect to Logan.

"How did *you* do?" he asked.

Shrugging, she said, "Not much. Small lead. Maybe."

Dix and Luke came in next, Luke carrying a small black box in his arms like it was a new puppy. Max cocked an eye; the "puppy" seemed to be smoking from one end.

Luke looked up, tears in his black eyes. "This little box has broken every code I've ever turned it loose on."

"It doesn't look so good," Max said.

"No, it doesn't," Dix admitted. "We've what you might call a setback."

"Yeah?"

Luke, nodding, said, in the voice of a school kid who'd been beaten up on by a playground bully, "Logan's computer burned up my codebreaker."

"What?"

"Burned it up! Tied it into some kind of loop that kept going faster and faster until the poor baby finally overheated and just . . . burned up."

Max grunted a laugh. "Logan's a smart cookie."

"I thought my little box was pretty smart, too," Luke said, walking off with the smoking box, possibly to bury it.

"So you got nothing?" Max asked.

Dix shrugged. "Does a migraine count?"

Mole came in next, his head down. "Bling says Logan swore him to secrecy."

"Maybe I should go talk to him," Max said.

"Can I watch?" Alec asked.

But Mole was shaking his head, saying, "I don't think he knows anything, anyway. Bling's a pretty tough character—and he'd just go into a yoga trance while we pulled out his toenails with pliers or some-thin'."

Max said, "I have the pliers."

"Not worth the trouble," Mole said, and relighted his stogie. "Anyway, Bling said Logan never let him know that kind of info—figured Bling was too obvious a target, and if somebody did torture him or use truth serum on 'im or somethin', best Bling not know anything important."

Joshua straggled in last, carrying a pillowcase like a sack. Whatever the shaggy transgenic was lugging looked heavy.

"What did you find, Big Fella?"

"Nothin', Little Fella. Sorry."

Max felt sick to her stomach. She had the name of the town, and that was a start; but there could be ten thousand or more people in Appleton. What were they going to do, go door to door?

"If you didn't find anything," Alec asked, "what's in the pillowcase? Kibble?"

Joshua shrugged. "Not kibble, Alec." He gazed mournfully at Max. "Logan had some of Father's books out, so I brought them along. But I couldn't find anything else."

"Let's see the books," she said.

Joshua emptied the pillowcase onto the map table, and the volumes clattered like big hailstones.

A dozen books lay in front of them. At Max's instructions, everybody picked one out and started flipping through the pages, in case Logan had made a stray note in one of the margins. Max knew Logan well enough to realize he didn't trust his own memory—bright as he was, Logan still felt the need for pneumonic devices, so he was always leaving himself cryptic little notes.

The third book Max picked up was *Gulliver's Travels*, a hard-back edition of the classic satire, similar to one she'd had when she was living in the projection booth at Mann's Chinese Theater in Los Angeles. On the inside of the cover, next to where Father had inscribed it for Joshua, Max saw a doodle—a pencil-drawn little apple . . .

Appleton?

Had Logan, looking for a new name for Ray White, absently plucked one from a book? *This* book?

"We have a name or two to try," she said, trying to keep the excitement out of her voice.

She could stand the despair . . . It was the hope . . .

"Get me an uplink," she said. "We're going to see if the tiny town of Appleton, Washington, has a 'Gulliver' family, or maybe a 'Swift,' or even 'Lemuel' . . ."

"Max," Alec said, "you're grasping for straws . . ."

"And if we come up blank, we try every other

'Appleton' in the U.S. and Canada . . . Alec, grasping at straws is the only way to find a needle in a haystack."

With night falling, they commandeered Logan's car and were on the road toward the upstate hamlet of Appleton.

It had been easier than she had thought to locate Ray White. She just needed the right cryptic clues and a little insight into Logan and, oh yes, some luck; if a man named Moody hadn't given her Jonathan Swift's great book to read, years ago, they would not have this chance tonight to save Logan Cale.

Accompanied by Alec, Mole, and Joshua, Max drove through Seattle, using her old Jam Pony ID and claiming to have an emergency delivery. When the sector cops asked why it took four messengers to deliver one package, she jerked her thumb toward Joshua and Mole in the backseat.

"It's radioactive, with a potential leak," she said. "The transgenics are the only ones who are able to deal with it without dying."

The prospect of leaking radioactivity was plenty to convince every sector cop they encountered. Max and crew and their hazardous materials were allowed free passage. And once they cleared the checkpoints in the city, the rest was easy.

As they whipped down the highway, Mole had the wheel with a foot mashed down on the gas. Max rode shotgun, studying the map even in the dark, her cat eyes still able to make out the details. In the back, Joshua and Alec tried to catch some rest and the two of them leaned into each other as they slept, a boy and his dog . . . his really, really big dog.

Glancing over her shoulder, Max wished she could take a photo of the two sleeping warriors; it wasn't often she was presented with an image that was on the one hand warm and fuzzy, and on the other, perfect blackmail material.

Leave it to Logan Cale to come up with a literary alias for Ray White. Lemuel Gulliver traveled between two worlds, and so had Ray. Max remembered the book fondly from nights when it lulled her to sleep back at the Chinese. That book had been the one possession she regretted leaving behind in Los Angeles when she'd left, seeking Seth in Seattle.

Max missed her Chinese Clan family, Moody, Tippett, and especially Fresca; but they were dead, and revenge, such as it was, had been taken. The book, though—*Gulliver's Travels*—had stayed with her. Like memories of a childhood she'd never had, the book was always part of her.

She wondered if Logan had remembered her talking about the book when he picked Ray White's alias. If so, she'd planted the very clue she'd been able to interpret; the irony of that made her smile, a little. Maybe she would ask Logan about that when she saw him . . .

If she saw him.

The first order of business would be convincing the boy's aunt—now using the name Sara Gulliver and pretending to be the boy's mother—to help them. Max knew the woman would be reluctant to get involved, and risk the boy's safety; but perhaps to help rescue the man who had saved both her life and Ray's, she might consider it.

Once Max had the name, tracking the pair down on the Internet had been surprisingly easy. The Internet was getting better every day, more and more like the heyday in the early '00s, especially here on the left coast, farther from the reach of the Pulse.

Things were less screwed up here than on the East Coast, and businesses were making a comeback. Even though that pirate Jared Sterling had made millions bilking the public as he rebuilt the Internet, his death had signaled a new freedom to build; and the Internet was playing a large role in renewing commerce within the United States, if mostly out West.

The Internet also provided more information than it had at any time since the Pulse. Now, Max not only knew where the Gullivers lived but where Sara worked, where Lem went to school, and even what kind of grades the boy was getting—not surprisingly, considering his genes, straight A's.

"Town," Mole said back over his shoulder.

The two in the back stirred, saw the position they were in, and instantly slid to the far sides of the vehicle, each looking toward the front to see if anyone had noticed them. They glanced quickly at each other, gave a little nod that signaled they didn't think the others had seen, then they both sighed in relief.

"You lovebirds have a nice nap?" Mole asked.

Joshua glared at the lizard man, and Alec offered a couple of short words in response.

Within minutes they were pulling up in front of the Gulliver house, a white two-story clapboard dating to the first half of the twentieth century, resting on a well-tended sloping lawn, a large ash tree in the front yard, and they could glimpse some other big trees out back. It was after dark but early in the evening, yet no lights were on inside the house. Max wondered if the Gullivers were out to dinner or visiting a neighbor.

They could be anywhere, doing anything, blithely leading an idyllic small-town life, unaware of the storm swirling around young Ray White . . . that is, Lem Gulliver.

And all the transgenic team could do was wait for them to come home. Leaning against her side of the car, Max looked up at the house. She hoped the Gullivers wouldn't be gone all evening. She wanted to get back to Terminal City; getting the boy was only the beginning—a strategy to defeat White, and return Logan, had yet to be developed.

She was about to turn and ask Mole a question when she saw a sudden illumination in a second floor window, as if someone had taken a picture with a flashbulb . . .

. . . and Max was running toward the house and up the lawn even before she heard the report.

The X5 knew a muzzle flash when she saw it.

"Gun!" she yelled over her shoulder, but the others were in action already, too, even as she saw another flash, and they heard a second report from upstairs, terrible momentary thunder in the otherwise quiet night.

She shouldered through the locked door and on inside, Joshua on her heels, Mole and Alec taking off around back to block the shooter's retreat to the rear.

The stairs were immediately to the right, and she hit the fourth step just as a head peeked around the corner at the top, a stocking-capped head that looked like it belonged on the body of a big man, which it did. He stepped forward, showing off a linebacker's frame and, more important, a nine millimeter automatic in his right hand.

Taking the rest of the stairs in a single bound, she leaped, landed at the top on one side and swung her leg around, her foot catching the man in the face. He backed up but neither flinched nor dropped the gun.

Shit, she thought, noting the lack of reaction; any normal human would've dropped in pain. *A Familiar!*

Had a squad of cultists been sent to guard Ray? And if so, why didn't Ames White know where his son was?

Pressing her advantage, she punched him six quick times, backing him up toward the door of the room from which they had seen the gunshot flash, outside.

And if the Familiars were guarding Ray, who the hell were they shooting at in that bedroom?

The Familiar brought the pistol up again, and this time Max grabbed his arm and spun, the barrel of the pistol pointing directly at Joshua, who had followed her up the stairs but was now facing her.

At the last second Joshua dodged to the right as the Familiar pulled the trigger two times, the shots blowing through the front wall of the house and into the night.

Max heard Joshua growling, but there was no way to let him by, and she didn't want to, anyway . . . not until she'd disarmed the Familiar. She crashed the man's arm down on her shoulder and heard a satisfying crack as his arm broke at the elbow, the pistol slipping from his grip and *thunk*ing on each stair as it bounced to the bottom like a heavy Slinky. The Familiar made no noise when his arm snapped—pain just didn't seem to register on these bastards—swinging the limp limb like a whip. The open other hand caught her on the side of the head and sent her tumbling down the stairs, as if following the gun.

Somehow, Joshua got past her, grabbed the Familiar around the waist and forced him toward the far end of the wall. Rolling into a combat stance, Max rushed back up the stairs and pushed her way through the closed door into the bedroom. The window was smashed and any Familiar that had been in here was gone.

All that remained were Sara Gulliver and her "son" Lemuel, aka Ray White.

And they were both dead.

From the hall, Joshua roared with rage, then Max heard another nasty crunching sound . . . then silence.

Heartsick, she spun into the hall and found Joshua, blood running from a wound in his shoulder. The Familiar hung limply in the Big Fella's arms, head lolling like a Christmas goose with its neck broken.

Forcing herself back into the bedroom, Max gaped at the horrifying sight before her. On the floor, their hands tied behind their backs, gags in their mouths, the woman and the child both lay facedown, a single bullet hole in the back of each of their heads.

Executed.

Alec and Mole came pounding in from outside.

"Bastard got away," Mole said. "We were around back, he went out the front! He was one fast son of a . . ." The lizard man's voice trailed off as he took in the bodies on the floor. "Oh, God."

Pushing by him, Alec saw the carnage. Shaking his head, he turned away.

Bending down, Max touched Ray's face. It was still warm.

Why would the Familiars kill Ames White's son?

This made no sense at all to her! Not only had they killed White's boy, they had taken the only bargaining chip she had left. She stroked the child's head, his hair, and she wept.

She wanted to be tough.

But with the dead child, and the realization that Logan was going to die—and that there was nothing she could do to prevent it—these things and every other thing she hadn't cried about for all those years, all the way back to Manticore, came pouring out.

She knelt there, one hand on Ray's head, the other on her forehead as she wept. Tears ran freely, her body wracked with sobs.

"Let it out, Little Fella," the gentle giant said, kneeling beside her now.

Max wondered if she ever could, though—there was too much to let out, there had been so many wrongs, so much pain, with no end in sight. Was this the normal life she'd hoped for, this endless parade of pain?

At least little Ray White could sleep through it all—his pain, his travels, over.

Chapter Eight
JOSHUA FIT THE BATTLE

Eventually, as Max's sobs began to abate, Alec stepped forward and placed a hand on her shoulder.

Max glanced back at the X5, surprised by the gentleness of the gesture and the genuine sorrow on the handsome face. She swallowed, nodding to him a small "Thank you" for his concern.

His hand was still on her shoulder as Max—making no effort to rise—looked down again at Ray, as she continued to run a soothing hand through the boy's hair, her fingers inches away from moist, matted blood.

He looked just as she remembered him, a bright-looking boy, hair cut short like his father's, the color more the blond of his late mother's. Rather small for his age—some of White's fellow cultists had doubted the boy had it in him to belong in their "exalted" ranks—he might have been asleep, but for the hole in his head.

"Max," Alec said, "we gotta haul—somebody in the

"Okay," Max said. "Joshua, can you carry this guy?"

Still ignoring the knife in his shoulder, Joshua responded by reaching down, grabbing the corpse and tossing it over his good shoulder, like a sack of grain.

Alec's eyes widened and his mouth dropped like a trapdoor. "What the hell . . . ?"

"Mole," Max said, no-nonsense, "get the boy. Wrap him in a white sheet."

Mole's cigar fell out of his mouth. "No freakin' way! What kinda ghoulish shit—"

Max thumped the lizard man's chest with two fingers. "The kid is dead. When I said we wouldn't trade the boy for Logan, I meant a *breathing* Ray White. It's not going to hurt that poor boy now, taking a ride with us."

Alec, his eyes as horrified as they were huge, stepped up. "Max, have you completely lost it? This plan *beyond* sucks!"

She latched onto Alec's shoulder with a hand that was nowhere near as gentle as his had been. "Toughen up, girls! . . . Ames White's going to want proof of what happened here. That it was the Familiars who betrayed him, not us!"

"You mean, the boy . . . his body . . . is evidence," Mole said, picking up his cigar.

"You're goddamn right he's evidence!" a wild-eyed Alec said as the sirens grew more insistent. "You're gonna put two corpses in our car, what, in the trunk?"

"That's the idea," Max said.

"And if we get stopped by the cops," Alec said, "how do we explain that?"

"Firmly," she said. "Mole, Alec—do it . . . or bail. If you're not prepared to follow my lead, *right now*—bail."

Alec swallowed and sighed . . . and nodded his commitment. Mole was already heading back into the bedroom, to prepare the small sad package.

And Max was no longer a distraught young woman, nor was Joshua an upset oversize teddy bear—all four of the transgenics made up a highly trained combat team again (Thank you, Colonel Lydecker, Max thought, for small favors), and nothing the Familiars and/or Ames White had to throw at them was going to stop them.

They were out of the Gulliver house in less than a minute, and—with the two bodies, the boy's sheet-wrapped, tucked in the trunk of Logan Cale's car—they took off, but carefully, Mole scrupulously obeying the speed limit. Though the sirens increased, Max and her unlikely teammates never even saw a squad car.

When they hit the edge of town without being stopped, Mole sped up a little, but he kept within a few miles of the limit.

"Where to?" the driver asked at last. "Or are we just gonna cruise around with our passengers until they start gettin' ripe?"

"Three Tree Point," Max said.

Mole shot her a look.

She gave him a sharp glance back. "Do I stutter?"

"Why in the hell?"

"Someone we need to talk to."

Alec leaned forward from the backseat. "You need to talk to somebody on Lyman Cale's estate, right?"

She half turned. "Not bad, Alec."

Mole, not taking his eyes off the road, said, "What?"

Alec explained. "There's no other reason to go to Three Tree Point than to steal a boat and head for the Cale mansion."

Max smiled grimly. "See, Alec? You're not just a pretty face."

"And you really do have a plan that doesn't suck," he said with his own grim smile.

Catching up with them, Mole said, "So, then . . . the guy in the trunk who needs a chiro—he's from Cale's, right?"

She nodded, and quickly filled them in.

"So," Mole said, "since Joshua killed Tweedledee, and since Tweedledum got away from us . . . they're probably gonna be waitin' for us."

"With bells on," Max said.

A grin creased Mole's reptilian features. "Just think how sick they're gonna look when we kick their asses, anyway."

With the exception of Joshua, they all smiled at Mole's bravado. Max only hoped it wasn't misplaced.

She had fought Familiars before and was amazed at how much pain they absorbed with seemingly no response. She had seen Ames White shoot himself in the arm and not even flinch. Two of them had ganged up on her when she tried to free Ray the first time, and no matter how hard she'd fought, they hadn't even seemed to notice her efforts.

She also had no idea how much of the security staff on Sunrise Island belonged to the Familiars. The burly boys, Otto and Franz, were obvious snake cult candidates. But Familiars didn't always look like top physical specimens fresh from the gym. White himself was of rather average build, and yet in combat against him, she'd had plenty of trouble.

Granted, she and Joshua and other transgenics had scored a victory over White's snake-cult SWAT team that time at Jam Pony; but every fight with the Familiars had proven to be arduous, to say the least—you had to beat them into unconsciousness or cripple them or kill them to take them out.

She wondered what the four of them could manage if the Familiars seriously outnumbered them on Lyman Cale's private island.

"Let's pull over," she said when she felt they were safely out of town, "and get Joshua patched up before we do anything else."

"Joshua is fine," Joshua said, the knife hilt sticking out of him like a slot-machine handle.

"Shut-up, Joshua," Max said.

"Shut-up?"

"Yes."

"Okay, Max."

"Good."

"Max?"

"Yes, Joshua?"

"Are you mad at me?"

"No, Joshua."

"Because you said 'shut-up,' and Joshua thought—"

"Shut-up, Joshua."

"Yes, Max."

Hunkered over the wheel, Mole said, "I know a place not far from here. Nice and private."

Max didn't even want to know how Mole knew about places between Appleton and Seattle. Sometimes she had to remind herself that the transgenics hadn't all moved directly from Manticore to Terminal City.

After pulling off the highway and onto a ramp, then onto a two-lane road from there, Mole took them a good mile from the four-lane before he turned into a field on a tractor-access lane and stopped the car behind a stand of apple trees, ravaged by the recent cold spell; the skeletal trees remained thick enough to block any view of them from the highway, and one of them gave Max a place to sit Joshua down and prop him up, while she did a quick triage.

"Mole, you got your lighter?" she asked.

He nodded.

"Gonna need it. Got a knife?"

Another nod.

Alec shook his head and said to Mole, "What if she'd asked you for a ham sandwich?"

"How do you know I don't have one in my back pocket?" Mole asked the X5. "Anyway, Manticore did share their motto with the Boy Scouts, 'member." He gave Alec a little three-fingered salute. "Be prepared."

Alec gave Mole a one-fingered salute.

"Heat the knife blade," Max said. "When I pull this thing out, I'm gonna want to cauterize the wound."

Alec smirked. "You can take the girl out of Manticore, but you can't take Manticore out of the girl."

Joshua looked a little dubious, sitting there with his back against an apple tree, the moon illuminating his canine features with a lovely ivory cast. The temperature seemed to be slowly rising. Mole moved the flame over the blade of his knife, and Max could see Joshua staring at it, his eyes growing wider with each passing second.

When the blade glowed red, Max went to work.

She started with the knife in Joshua's shoulder. "You ready, Big Fella?"

He gulped and said, "Ready, Little Fella," and Max jerked the knife out of his shoulder. Joshua let out a piteous howl, his eyes growing wide, and he unconsciously started shaking his head as she dropped one knife and held out her hand for Mole to give her the heated one.

His eyes glued to the glowing blade, Joshua whimpered like a puppy.

"Hey," she said, "who loves you?"

"Y-Y-You d-do?"

"That's right, Big Fella."

"Joshua loves Max, too, Little Fella."

And with his eyes on hers, she grinned, he grinned, then she pressed the hot blade into his wound, and the werewolf howl that roared from deep within him reminded Max of Joshua's brother Isaac and the screams of pain he elicited when in the throes of his homicidal rage. Surprisingly, the two brothers didn't sound all that different . . . which was enough to give Max a little shiver.

She withdrew the knife and, under the flame from Mole's lighter, inspected her work.

"Looking good," she said.

Joshua gave her a frown that said he wasn't as impressed, and that pulling the "Little Fella" limb from limb may have crossed his mind. "Max hurt Joshua."

"Max had to . . . for your own good, Big Fella. Hey, it's going to be all right now. Rest for a little while. I'll be right here."

He eyed the knife warily until she handed it back to Mole.

"Rest, I said," she scolded.

Leaving the beast man to sleep against the tree, the others moved off a little ways and found places to sit on the ground.

Max looked up at a million stars. It was a different sky out here, somehow—more stars, brighter moon, reminding her of the night the twelve of them had escaped from Manticore. It had been a long trip since then, her only goal to find a home, to settle down. Now, in Terminal City, she had a home, all right; but being out here, on the run again, reminded her of how claustrophobic the city had become.

Mole yanked an automatic pistol fitted with a silencer out of his belt and set it on the ground in front of him.

"Where did you pull that out of?" she asked.

Alec smirked. "Are you sure you wanna know?"

Mole tilted his head in the direction of Appleton.

"From the Gulliver house. Belonged to our no-neck passenger, in the car."

Max hated guns. They all knew it; but she also was savvy enough, pragmatic enough, to know that a little firepower could make a difference tonight. And if Mole wanted to go that way, she had no right to try to stop him—not when she was asking him to follow her through the gates of Hell.

"With what we're about to do," Mole said apologetically, "I thought it might come in handy."

She nodded, looking away.

"You cool with it?" Mole asked.

"No."

"You want me to toss it?"

"Do what you have to."

"I hate to bring this up," Alec said to her. "But what exactly is your plan?"

Mole grinned. "Step one, find these assholes; step two, kick their asses."

"Max," Alec said, "*is* that your plan?"

Cigar jutting threateningly, Mole asked, "What part didn't you get? Step one, or step two?"

Max cut in. "This isn't about revenge, remember. It's about kidnapping."

Obviously not sure he was following her, Alec asked, "Logan's kidnapping, you mean?"

"No. This time *we're* the kidnappers."

Alec raised an eyebrow. "Well, I guess that's a step up from your last assignment—body-snatching."

Max ignored that. "Our target is Lyman Cale's majordomo, Franklin Bostock. He's the key. Nothing happens within that compound without his approval.

Stands to reason, he's either a Familiar or in their pocket—he very likely sent those two snake-cult goons to kill that child."

"And his mother," Alec said.

Max shook her head. "The mother was just collateral damage."

Mole said, "What you're sayin' is, don't ice the Bostock dude."

"Bingo," Max said. "His sleazy self, we need alive."

"You think?" Alec asked. "We're hauling two stiffs around, already—what's one more?"

Max didn't know whether to be irritated by Alec or amused—Alec, the guy who always cut corners, who always looked for the angle, was suddenly the conservative of the group. A squeaky-clean Alec was somehow a frightening thought. She was about to give him some good-natured hell about it when her cell phone chirped in her pocket.

She pulled it out and punched a button. "Go for Max."

"Do you have my son yet?"

Ames White.

As always, that voice sent a chill through her.

"Working on it," she said. "We know where he is."

"Clock's ticking, 452. Only two days to go. You're going to do the right thing, aren't you?"

"Doing my best."

"Not playing games? Why do I think you already have my son?"

"I'm not playing games. But I promise you, we will deliver him."

Somehow, even though this was Ames White, it sickened her to lie to the boy's parent—*not lie, really, like Original Cindy said . . . a sin of omission, not commission*—when the child lay bundled in a white-sheet shroud in the trunk of a nearby car.

"I want Ray to wake up Christmas morning in a brand new world," White's processed voice said confidently into her ear. *"Make it happen, 452, and your friend Logan might live to see the new year, that brand new world . . . and we can put our differences behind us."*

What the hell did that mean, a "brand new world"?

"I'm cooperating, White. Working to make it happen."

"I hope you are. Now, don't screw this up, 452—your friend is counting on you."

"Let me talk to him."

White laughed mirthlessly. *"I will, when you let me talk to Ray."*

"Can't right now."

"Puts us in the same boat, doesn't it? Well, then . . ."

Were they in the "same boat"? Was Logan dead—as dead as Ray White?

"If I don't talk to Logan," she said, "no deal."

"Do you really think you're in a position to negotiate, 452? I have to say, for all our differences, I do admire your confidence. You have a certain . . . presence."

"Yeah, well. Girl's gotta try."

"Try this, 452—like it or not, we're both going to have to show a little faith here."

"Faith?"

"*Not an attribute either of us would ever likely be accused of having in abundance . . . but in this situation, it would seem required. Comes down to this: you hold up your end, and I'll hold up mine.*"

"Why is it I have trouble believing you'll hold up your end?"

"*Ah. That's where the faith comes in.*"

The phone clicked dead in her ear. She looked at it for a long moment, and resisted the urge to fling it against a tree.

"What was that about?" Alec asked.

"Just Ames White, busting my chops," she said. "What else is new?"

"Does he know about Ray?"

"I don't think so. I suppose it's possible . . . evil bastard like White. But my reading of this is, he really does want his son back . . . may even 'love' him, in his sicko Ames White way."

"I wouldn't know much about parental love," Alec said. "Hard to bond with a test tube."

"I hear you," she said. "But my gut says, White is a victim here, too—his son was murdered. And, dark as it may sound, that may be to our advantage."

Mole chomped on the cigar, frowning. "How the hell . . . ?"

"If we can convince White that the Familiars killed his boy, and sold him out, then it maybe takes the heat off us, gets us Logan back, and turns White against the cult."

Alec snorted a laugh. "Oh, yeah—that would be a

nice bonus. Get Logan back, *and* take down the snake cult."

"I'm just sayin'—he's been betrayed, and I don't think he knows it. White thinks we haven't gotten to Ray yet, and has no idea that his son's dead. On the other hand, if White finds out the boy's dead before we can convince him it wasn't our fault . . ."

Grim nods from both Alec and Mole completed the thought.

They got moving.

Mole stuffed the pistol back in his belt, Alec and Max helped a slightly groggy Joshua back into the car, and they made for Seattle, Max trying not to dwell on the bodies in the trunk.

At Three Tree Point, where security was lax, to say the least, they helped themselves to a motorboat—Max thought it might be the same one from her previous trip to Sunrise Island. The car with its trunkful of corpses was lying low in a dim corner of the parking lot. They would have the cover of darkness for their approach, but—true to the island's name—they would arrive just as the sun peeked over the horizon. That didn't make Max feel any better, but there was nothing to be done about it.

As they droned across Puget Sound, Max laid out a plan of action for taking the island. None of her crew questioned any of her strategy; no jokes, no doubts—a commando squad ready to serve their leader.

Again using a rubber raft, Max and her transgenic trio hit the beach just as the sky lightened in the east. Max was mildly surprised that no one was waiting for them at the shore. Using hand signals, she communicated that they should spread out and approach the house in pairs.

As usual, Joshua went with her to the left, while Mole accompanied Alec to the right. She knew the security force numbered at least twenty, and she hoped her assumption that only a handful of them were Familiars was correct. Twenty ordinaries would barely raise a sweat for either pair of transgenics; the Familiars, though, they might be another story . . .

Again, that brutal battle against White's SWAT team on the second floor of Jam Pony popped into her mind, and she shook her head a little.

Twenty Familiars might be more than the four of them could handle.

She turned to glance at Joshua for reassurance as they made their way through the woods. The Big Fella held his nose in the air, sniffing. He pointed slightly ahead of them and to their left, then held up three fingers.

No sooner had Joshua made this gesture than a trio of Cale guards in their black TAC fatigues stepped into their path, automatic weapons leveled at the pair. No dogs tonight—except Joshua, of course. She noted that the three were paunchy, probable ordinaries.

Immediately, instinctively, she saw Bostock's plan.

The first wave would be ordinaries, the Familiars staying close, protecting their leader and his treasure, that valuable vegetable, Lyman Cale.

As per plan, Max and Joshua raised their hands, giving off an aura of surrender. Almost imperceptibly, their captors relaxed . . .

. . . and in the next instant Max moved forward, in a blur, disarming all three before they could start squeezing a trigger, much less fire a shot; and she tossed their weapons into the woods with twig-breaking thuds.

Simultaneously, Joshua had blurred forward himself, moving right behind her, cracking two side-by-side skulls together, knocking the guards out, while Max dispatched the third with a kick to the head that didn't quite kill the man, though when he awoke from this sleep, he'd likely have the worst hangover a man who hadn't been drinking ever had.

And the two transgenics pressed on.

On the other side of the island, Mole and Alec faced a similar challenge.

Mole had spotted the three guards early on, and signaled to Alec that they should get around the trio and come up behind them. His plan worked beautifully and the three guards were dispatched almost before they knew they were attacked.

The best part, Mole thought, was the fact that he and Alec now each carried an HK53 submachine gun. They would stay silent as long as possible, but at some point Mole expected there would be more serious trouble.

Still, he kept up his cigar-chewing bravado. Careful to keep his voice low, Mole growled, "And Max was worried about these punks?"

Alec shrugged. "She's a girl. She's a worrier."

They edged forward through the woods and had

managed another two hundred yards when five more guards surrounded them.

"Thought you had our back," Mole said.

"Thought I did," Alec replied.

Stepping forward, one of the guards said, "Put the weapons down . . . softly . . . carefully."

So much for having machine guns.

They both set their HK53s down, bending at the knees to do so; then the transgenics exploded into action . . .

Sidestepping the one who had given the order, Mole went for the guard to his left, launching himself and hitting the guard in the stomach with his shoulder. The guard let out a *whoomp*, as all the air in his lungs abandoned ship. Both guards toppled to the grass, Mole rolling away and jumping up just as the leader's gun barked twice. Mole dodged right and felt a bullet graze his left side, the other bullet striking the guard he'd knocked down in the forehead, as the man tried to rise.

That would leave a mark.

Spinning back the other way, Mole unleashed a vicious side kick that knocked the machine gun out of the leader's hand. From the corner of his eye, Mole saw Alec leap, kicking out in opposite directions, each foot connecting with the face of a guard.

Three down, two to go.

The leader stepped in and delivered a quick left jab, followed by an overhand right, rocking Mole. As the lizard man staggered back, the leader kicked him in the solar plexus, driving the air out of him, knocking him off a tree, and leaving him dazed in a pile on the ground at the base of the trunk.

Struggling to stay conscious, Mole got to his knees, expecting the leader to be on him at any second . . .

. . . but no attack came.

His vision cleared and he looked up to see that Alec—who had dispatched the fourth guard—now had the leader in a full nelson. Before Mole could get to his feet, though, the leader dropped to his knees, pulling Alec over the top and rolling toward Mole, who grunted as Alec struck him and knocked them both to the ground.

The transgenics rose as one and saw the leader scrambling for the machine gun Mole had knocked away. Both of them took off as if fired from cannons, coming up behind the leader, each grabbing an arm and using the man's own momentum against him as they sprinted toward a huge oak.

They passed on either side of the tree, the leader meeting the trunk face first with a sickening crunch, his arms slipping from their hands as his momentum abruptly stopped.

The leader stood facing the tree for a moment, as if it were a door that had been slammed in his face; then, with no more consciousness than the tree, he flopped back on the ground, his face a mask of blood, his mouth hanging open, several of his teeth broken. Guy probably wasn't dead, Mole thought, but definitely out of the game.

Alec asked, "You all right?"

Mole looked down at his left side, stained dark in

the half-light of dawn. "Never better," he said, not wanting to tell his friend that it hurt like hell.

"Like Max says," Alec said, "let's blaze."

And they were running.

A pang of worry shook Max when she heard the shots from the other side of the island.

She hoped the others were safe, but—soldier that she was—she couldn't afford to fret about it long. Off to their right she saw a five-man patrol just as they saw her. The guards were only about thirty yards away and their guns came up instantly.

"Guns!" she shouted. "Run!"

She'd already taken off.

Zigzagging, she could hear Joshua crashing through the woods behind her as bullets whizzed past, snapping branches, *thunk*ing into trees, the five automatic weapons sounding more like a hundred.

Max and Joshua sprinted on, running for all they were worth, ducking, weaving, dodging, the guards giving chase now but keeping up the barrage. Only the transgenics' special gifts kept them from being gunned down, and Max wondered how long their luck and skill would hold.

Then, suddenly, Joshua went down!

Max heard it and sensed it and turned to see, but she'd lost sight of him as she skirted the bullets still flying at her. Rolling to her right, she popped up to see Joshua throw one of the guards like a football, the man splatting into a tree and sagging to the earth.

Springing to her feet, Max rushed one who was so stunned he didn't even fire as she ran toward him, leaped and kicked, her boot connecting solidly with his face. Blood spewed from his broken nose as he went down, unconscious.

She got a glimpse of Joshua throwing another one into a tree, and that made three down . . .

Another one shot at her, but the bullets went wide right, as she instinctively dodged left. Jumping high, she somersaulted and came down at the feet of guard number four, who flinched just before she decked him with a right cross that knocked him cold.

She looked around for Joshua, found him, then her heart lurched as she realized the last guard had avoided hand-to-hand combat as he tracked his shot and the man now had Joshua zeroed in . . .

Max yelled a warning, but it came too late: the guard squeezed the trigger and fired a single round. Joshua's eyes met hers for the briefest fraction of an instant, still long enough to share love, surprise, forgiveness, thankfulness, everything in that one bit of a second . . .

. . . then the bullet *thwack*ed into the gentle giant's chest, and Joshua hurtled backward, his arms flying out, his eyes going wide, his mouth dropping open, but no sound came out and he disappeared into the brush.

In the next instant the shooter was turning toward where he'd heard Max yell.

She dove for cover, rolled, and—possessed by a burning rage . . . no soldier ever forgave another soldier for doing his duty—she blasted forward, blurring into a zigzagging ghost, the shooter always just missing her as he fired off the whole clip. When he went

empty, she swept his legs and dumped him on his ass.
As he tried to kick his way back to his feet, Max
caught him with a straight right that slowed the guard,
but didn't hurt him.

A Familiar.

"Good," Max said, and smiled a terrible smile.
"Time we found out just where your pain threshold
begins . . ."

He was a good six inches taller than her, and a good
fifty pounds heavier, and if the muscles bulging
through the fatigues were any indication, he was
probably a good deal stronger than her, too.

The man growled, but it got cut off by the boot she
planted in his chest. He backed up, then came forward trying to get in close, where his size would
give him an advantage. Max sidestepped him, back-
elbowed him in the head as he went by, then—as he
turned—she leapt and broke his nose with her boot.

Incensed now, he charged again.

This time she held her ground and—when he
hurled himself at her—Max simply went limp and
dropped.

As the guard flew over her, she caught him in the
throat with an uppercut. The guard sprawled onto the
forest floor. He rolled and tried to rise, but it was clear
he was losing momentum, his breathing ragged
through the blood-filled broken nose, even as he
choked from the last punch.

As he sat up, Max was on him again. Three quick
rights sent him back down, groggy. When he lifted his
head again, Max—tired of her new game, deciding
this snake-cult son of a bitch didn't need to suffer,

just die—took his skull in both hands and gave it a violent twist, breaking the man's neck like a celery stalk.

She let go of the head, and the limp dead form slumped to the ground.

She went off to look for Joshua and spotted him, spread-eagled about ten yards away, his eyes closed, his chest barely moving. She went to his side, knelt next to him and finally forced herself to look at the wound in his chest. To her surprise, she saw no blood on his coat.

Max steeled herself to lift it back, but then Joshua moaned, opened his eyes, blinked a few times, and in a strangled voice barely above a whisper, asked, "What happened, Little Fella?"

"You were shot, Big Fella."

"Took one for the team?"

". . . Afraid so."

Joshua swallowed thickly. "C-Cold."

She stripped off her leather vest and covered him with it as best she could.

He moaned, and it almost sounded like a death howl.

"Does it hurt?"

"Hurt," he repeated. "Like I got punched—hard."

His hand went to his chest and she tried to pull it away, but he was stronger. Reaching under the vest and inside his coat, he drew out something red, and for the briefest moment Max had a vision of him pulling out his own heart.

But what he had in his pawlike hand was a book . . .

. . . the hard-back copy of *Gulliver's Travels* she had used to find Ray White in Appleton.

Slowly, Joshua sat up and looked at the blood-colored volume with a neat entry wound in the cover that went almost all the way through. When he riffled the pages, the bullet tumbled out.

"Are you mad, Max?" he asked.

"Mad?"

"Joshua ruined Father's book."

Relief flooded through Max and she grabbed her monstrous friend in her arms and gave him a big hug.

"*Ow!*" he growled.

"Aw, did that hurt?" she asked. Pulling back and taking his face in her hands, she gave him a big, wet, sloppy kiss.

This time he didn't say anything, and when she let him go, a wide smile spread over his face. His eyes were glassy, and he wobbled for a moment.

Then he passed out.

"Big Fella," she said, and shook him.

He was dead to the world . . . but not dead, thank God.

Plenty left to do tonight, and now she had two or three hundred pounds of dog-boy transgenic to haul out of these woods.

Still, it was a hell of a lot better than leaving his dead furry body behind.

Chapter Nine
MEET THE NEW BOSS

Just twenty yards from the west side of the house, Mole and Alec huddled in the woods. Between them and the mansion lay the building's blue shadow, one last suggestion of night, even though ten minutes ago—on the other side of the massive, mausoleum-quiet building—the sun had broken through, bringing a not entirely welcome morning. And yet the chill of the night clung to them, as they squatted like oversize gnomes at the base of an oak.

"Where are they?" Mole asked, the reptilian face wrinkling with impatience. "What do you think? Should we go lookin' for 'em?"

"We should do what Max said," Alec said, "and wait."

"Mr. Frickin' Rule Book all of a sudden!"

Alec offered up his trademark smirk. "Is it my fault you ran out of smokes?"

Mole said nothing, just scowled.

Alec's smirk softened into a smile. "Relax, buddy. They'll be along."

"They musta heard the shots."

"Yeah—and we heard shots, too, remember? They maybe had a little trouble of their own."

"They maybe got iced."

"Maybe. But for now we wait."

Mole sighed heavily and settled in. "All right . . . but it'd be easier if I had a damn cigar."

"Life with you would be easier for *me* if you had a damn cigar . . . On the other hand, one look at the smoke and every goon and gun on the grounds'd be down on us."

"Yeah yeah yeah. It's a frickin' moot point, ain't it, smart-ass?"

A familiar female voice cut in: "Why don't you two try marriage counseling?"

Mole swung around and there was Max, coming up a path between trees, an arm around Joshua's waist, walking him along like he was drunk. To Alec, the smile on his friend's furry face was even a little dumber than usual, as well as inappropriate, considering the circumstances.

"What's up with Furballs?" Mole asked.

"He was shot," she said.

"What? Jesus—" Mole said, getting to his feet.

"You mean he was stabbed," Alec said, frowning, also getting up. "We all saw it, Max."

Helping the beast man along, she said, "That was then . . . this is now—but he'll be okay."

Mole was helping her with Joshua, who they walked over to the base of a tree, sitting him down.

"Where'd he get it?" the lizard man asked.

"In the front cover," she said, and quickly filled them in, finishing, "But he took the full impact of the slug—he's pretty shaken."

Joshua said, "Max kissed Joshua's oowwie," and grinned stupidly.

Alec and Mole exchanged lifted-eyebrow glances, then Alec said, "I don't even want to know."

Mole, amused, leaned toward Max, saying, "I got shot, too . . ." Then he puckered his lizard lips, as much as lizard lips could pucker, anyway.

And Max said, "You wish . . . Let's see it."

Mole showed her where the bullet had cut a crease in his vest and his side; the bleeding had stopped.

"Get over yourself!" she said. "I nick myself worse shavin' my legs."

Alec and Mole reflected on that image perhaps a beat too long, and Max snapped, "Can we get to business?"

Alec gestured through the trees. "I know about your cat-burglar background and all, Max—but how do you intend to get inside that dollhouse?"

The three-story antebellum mansion made, as before, an intimidating adversary, hedge in front, at least three windows on each floor on each side of the house . . .

"Windows," Max said.

"What about them?" Alec asked.

"That's our way in."

The X5 frowned. "We're not going to try to take out the alarm system? Those things'll be as wired as Sketchy on Saturday night. Not very subtle, Max."

"This from the guy who shot up the whole damned island on the way in."

Alec looked hurt. "*They* started it—anyway, I heard way more gunfire from your side."

She arched an eyebrow, a fist on a hip. "What, are you afraid alarms will alert them to our presence?"

Alec smirked humorlessly. "Well, maybe the gunshots already did that, yeah."

Mole cleared his throat.

They both turned to look at him.

"Anybody got a cigar?" he asked.

"No," Max said.

"Of course not," Alec said.

"No," Joshua said, and suddenly the Big Fella was standing next to them.

Mole made a mock-gracious "after you" gesture, half bowing. "Then can we just *do* this shit, please? So I can find my way back to civilization and some frickin' tobacco?"

They each came in from a different direction, breaking through a first-floor window—gloved hands punching a hole and reaching up to undo the latch—and rolling in, into a combat stance. No audible alarms were triggered, though silent ones would no doubt be registering in some security center.

Max had assigned Joshua—seeing as how he'd been both stabbed and shot recently—to go in on the west side; the window Max selected for him was toward the back, probably a study or den. Alec went around to the east side and came in through a dining room window. In the back, Mole barged into the kitchen, while in the front, Max rolled right into the living room. If you're gonna crash a party, Max thought, might as well really crash it . . .

Two guards waited for her, and when she came up, one hit her high in front while the other hit her low in back. She dropped, hit the floor hard, feeling like a gong somebody had sounded, and wondered for a moment if Alec might not have been right about being a little more circumspect in their entrance.

They were big and well-built, both with short, dark hair, and they wore black TAC fatigues. One was a few inches taller than his partner and had a short, crooked scar on his right cheek. But they were not smart: they should have immediately attacked a second time instead of waiting there, poised as if some invisible referee were counting Max out.

And of course Max wasn't about to be counted out . . .

Bouncing to her feet, she hit the nearest one, the scarred sucker, with a straight, powerful right, a punch that could have put a hole in a wall . . .

. . . and he didn't flinch.

Goddamn Familiars, she thought.

The other one kicked her in the back, but she was braced for a blow and took it well, only when she moved forward the scarred one karate-edged her in the stomach and doubled her over.

And unlike a Familiar, an X5 like Max—for all her superior attributes—could feel pain, all right . . .

Like an overeager dance partner, the scarred boy spun her around, jitterbug style, one hand on the scruff of her neck, the other on her backside, and ran her at the open window. With no more effort than it would take him to toss his jacket on a chair, the big man threw her through the window, over the hedge and into the yard, where she hit with a thud, rolled a couple of times, and stopped in a sprawl.

Standing in the window, the two Familiars grinned at her. Max got up, dusted herself off, and with a toss of the head, flung the hair from her eyes.

"Fellas—I been thrown outta better places, by better people."

Like an ugly family portrait in the frame of the broken window, the two guards just kept grinning at her. The scarred Familiar said, "You're always welcome here."

And he gestured with a little "com'ere" curl of the fingers.

Max smiled. "I think I will make another visit. Only this time, just for a change of pace—I'll kick *your* asses."

"Go," the scar-faced one said, and the rest of the phrase presumably would have been "for it," only Max didn't let him get that out. Instead, she launched herself back through the window, taking both men down with her in a wide generous embrace.

Max rolled off them, leaving the two startled men on their backs; then she landed nimbly on her feet and pirouetted, facing them, a woman possessed. They scrambled up even as her fists and feet flew in all directions, and—despite their incredibly high pain threshold—the Familiars could not withstand the one-woman onslaught. Though there were two of them, the guards were no match for this whirling dervish of a pissed-off X5.

The vast living room—the meager furnishings that remained sheet-covered and pressed up against the walls, like mute spectators—gave the three combatants plenty of space to maneuver on the hardwood floor.

The scarred one went down first, a vicious kick catching him on the side of the knee, tearing ligaments audibly. He didn't cry out, of course, but any lack of pain couldn't make up for the physical facts of life, and the leg gave out underneath him when he tried to attack her. He made one more sweeping attempt with his good leg, which she jumped as if skipping rope, and the aftermath of the guard's attempt was to present his chin at a nice angle; and Max clipped him with a straight, swift, hard right that turned out his lights.

The other one cartwheeled toward her, delivered a fast one-two and cartwheeled away.

"That looked pretty," she said. "Blow me another kiss, why don't you?"

And she waved for him to bring the shit again, and he did, this time cartwheeling in and kicking her first with his right, then his left foot, before cartwheeling away—she'd pulled back some, but he did catch her. She raised her gloved hand to her face, wiped a trickle of blood at the corner of her mouth, and waved for him to come back one more time.

This time he backflipped into a cartwheel, apparently hoping to confuse her, but Max was ready, and when he was braced for that split second on just one hand, she hit the floor in a baseball slide, knocked the guard's palm out from under him and dumped him on his head.

He jumped to his feet, only to find Max cartwheeling this time, right toward him; then she dropped into a roll and launched at him, her fist burying to the wrist in his crotch. He said nothing, his eyes bulging and watering as he bent over, obviously surprised by the intensity of the sensation.

"See?" Max said, with a demented little grin. "Some kindsa pain you just *can't* completely breed out of a guy . . ."

And she came up, delivering a hard head butt that broke the guard's nose, twin streams of blood erupting from either nostril as he went pitching back into the wall.

He bounced back at her, consumed with rage, blood and spittle flying as he roared toward her. At a fraction of the last moment, she sidestepped and the guard blasted through the middle unopened window, breaking glass raining all around as he came to rest over the sill, half in the room, half outside. It was as if he were taking a breather.

Then he stood, turned, blood dripping from several cuts as he stepped through the shattered glass. Coughing, he frowned and reached up and felt a huge shard protruding from his neck. He coughed again as if that might dislodge the scratching in his throat.

"Got a tickle?" Max asked. "Let me help."

She stepped forward, yanked the glass from the man's neck, and ducked, anticipating the arterial spray, which easily rose to the ceiling, where it painted a scarlet Jackson Pollock abstraction.

The Familiar's eyes went wide and his hands flew to his throat, but it was too late. Max drop-kicked him, sending him on through the window this time, to leave him outside to bleed to death. She knew it wouldn't take long.

Say what you will about Manticore, she thought, but science'll beat out pagan breeding rituals, any time.

She left the living room—and the drip-drip-drip of her opponent's blood off the ceiling—and went into the hall.

Joshua was emerging from the back of the house, in the midst of fighting another guard—obviously a Familiar (any human would be crushed by any one of Joshua's formidable blows)—backing the man slowly down the hall toward Max with a series of punches alternating between face and belly. The guard was putting up a good fight even though Joshua towered over him. Slowly, the battle neared her.

"Don't be cruel to animals," she said.

The guard turned, and she delivered a right cross that spun the man back toward Joshua, who caught him with a left hook. The Familiar's eyes closed and the guard melted to the floor.

"Hard to hurt them," Joshua said.

"They're like robots," Max said. "But when you shut off their electricity, they go down."

Joshua nodded, getting the concept.

"Check on Mole," she said. "I'll look for Alec."

They each took off in the direction from which they'd come, Joshua toward the back to find Mole in the kitchen, Max to the front to look for Alec, moving away from the living room. She ran into him at the bottom of the staircase, just as four Familiars opened fire with automatic weapons from above.

Both Max and Alec dove into the dining room, but they knew this sanctuary would last barely ten seconds. Already they could hear the guards thundering down the stairs. The room had a long table covered with two sheets and a dozen sheeted chairs, as if a banquet for ghosts was in sway. At the other end of the room, sharing the same wall as the door they'd used, another door led, presumably, to the kitchen.

Communicating with hand signals, they put a plan together—no time to decide whether it sucked or not, and anyway, it was a collaboration—then the X5s set it into action.

Alec took off for the back, while Max flattened herself against the wall, next to the near door.

When the first guard came in, Max jerked his gun out of his hand, and pulled him to her. As she did, a second guard fired at them, killing the guard Max held in front of her, a human shield.

Alec—having slipped out the door at the back of the dining room—came up the hall from the kitchen, Mole on one side of him and Joshua on the other, and the three of them waded into the remaining guards, just as Max discarded her dead shield and attacked the nearest opponent, using the butt of the commandeered weapon as a club, knocking him unconscious and to the floor in a pile.

Within seconds all the three guards were down, likely out for the rest of the day, if not dead. None of the three transgenics gave that a thought, not even the compassionate Joshua—these four were soldiers, bred by Manticore for combat, and soldiers did not linger over the casualties they'd created, shedding tears.

"You all right?" Alec asked Max.

"I feel good . . . You two?"

Mole said, "This is fun. If I had a frickin' smoke, my life would be a song."

Joshua said, "I'm alive, too, Little Fella."

"Stay that way, Big Fella," she said. "Let's get upstairs then—I'll take the point . . . Mole, you ride drag."

Nodding, they fell into line and paraded up the stairs, their eyes everywhere—another wave of guards, coming up behind them, would be a bad thing . . .

There were six bedrooms on the second floor and, Max supposed, probably an equal number on the third floor, though she had never been up there. Using hand signals, she sent Mole and Alec on upstairs, while she and Joshua checked the rooms on this floor, starting at the end farthest from Lyman Cale's bedroom.

They found nothing—no further guards, no guests, no Franklin Bostock—and had just arrived outside Lyman's door when the other two came down from the third floor and signaled that they had struck out up there as well.

They fanned out, Max in the lead again, Alec and Joshua on either side behind her, Mole off to one side, watching their backs.

Max opened the door. Stepped in.

Lyman Cale still lay in the bed; if possible, he

seemed even smaller, as if he'd shrunk further, a withered rind lost in a white nightshirt, cables coming in and out of him, keeping Logan's uncle alive, technically at least—as the surrounding monitors and gizmos attested.

Franklin Bostock—again in a black blazer, white shirt with no tie, and gray slacks—stood on the far side of the bed near Cale's head. He appeared calm, and their entry into the room seemed to barely register on him.

Alec and Joshua came in and spread out again behind Max.

"Thought you'd be back, Ms. Guevera," Bostock said, his voice detached, even cold.

But Max's voice was frigid. "Ray White."

Bostock looked up at her, unimpressed. "What of him?"

"He was an eleven-year old boy."

Bostock shrugged. "You know what they say about omelets."

"Is that what the boy is to you? *Was* to you? A broken egg?"

"You're a soldier, Ms. Guevera. All wars have their casualties. I imagine you've cut quite a swath through my men, coming this far."

"Wars? Casualties?" She took a menacing step forward. "Those things I know about . . . I also know about atrocities. Why? Why an innocent child?"

She took another step, and a small caliber pistol revealed itself in Bostock's hand.

And it was pointed at the head of Lyman Cale, not that that comatose figure had any realization of it.

"Take another step," he said, "and there will be another casualty in this war." A smile spread, like a terrible rash, across his bland face. "You might make it before I blow Lyman's brains—what's left of them—all over this pillow. But I doubt it."

She just stood there.

Bostock's eyes met hers. "You're still considering it, though, aren't you? Go ahead. Make your move—you may find me a more formidable adversary than you might imagine . . . And then you can explain to Logan Cale how you got his uncle killed."

The thought of what had happened to Seth because of Logan flitted across her mind, and in that moment what this sadistic son of a bitch had just said triggered an epiphany in Max.

Logan wouldn't have intentionally put Seth in danger—not any more than Logan would have done with her, when she accepted missions. It was always her choice, and it would have been the same for her sib. And the truth was, Seth liked taking risks even more than Alec or Zack.

Max understood why Logan had lied now. That is, she understood his act of omission, not commission . . .

If this situation went sideways, as it very well might at any moment, there would be no way in hell she could ever explain to Logan, no way she could bear to tell him, if she were to cause him to lose his uncle, the last relative of his on the planet who had ever seemed to care about him . . .

Bostock's voice grew sharp. "Your two playmates—on their knees. Hands behind their necks."

She could feel Alec and Joshua looking at her, and she turned to them, nodded once, and they complied, dropping as if in prayer, elbows winged as hands locked behind heads.

"You seem to think you're going somewhere," Max said.

Bostock nodded. "Out of here, for a start."

"How exactly?" Max crossed her arms. "You really think we're just going to let you through? Or are you gonna haul ol' Lyman out of bed and yank those tubes out of him and use him as a hostage? I'd pay to see that."

Bostock turned a bit and trained the pistol on Max. "Ms. Guevera . . . *you're* my hostage. And I think you'll comply—after all, accompanying me will be your only chance, however faint, of rescuing Logan Cale."

"And why is that?"

"Because I'll be taking you to where he's being held."

Max froze. "Then . . . you knew White's plan all along! You were *part* of it."

Bostock said, "Familiars do get . . . familiar. We share many things with each other—it's a brotherhood, after all."

"Yeah, like Cain and Abel." She shook her head. "If you knew what White was up to—that he planned to use me to get Ray back—why did you interfere with it? Why kill that boy?"

The man's eyes flared. "What, and allow Ames White to consolidate his power with the Conclave? I don't think so."

Her head was spinning. "How could a kid like that consolidate White's power?"

Bostock sighed, as if he were dealing with a child. "Ames White had hopes and dreams for his son—and there is a small but powerful faction among the Conclave who took the youngster's potential seriously. Others of us considered that boy weak—his mother an ordinary who betrayed us, his father a failure, the whole family nothing but a negative influence to our goals . . . Let's just say I removed a small problem."

She let out a bitter laugh. "So, for all your posing . . . you and this Conclave are really no better than the ordinaries, are you?"

Bostock looked baffled, and offended.

"Petty jealousy," she said. "Nothing more than petty jealousy cost that boy his life."

"Petty?" The word seemed to explode out of Bostock. Suddenly the calm bureaucrat was a seething demon. "It was White's family that burdened the Conclave with you transgenics in the first place! White's father—this Sandeman, you consider him *your* father don't you, all of you?—Sandeman lost his nerve, and now we have you mutated rabble to deal with. That family must be made to pay!"

Max frowned. "What is the Conclave's obsession with Sandeman and the transgenics? . . . What possible threat could we be to you and your twisted goals?"

In an instant, Bostock was the calm bureaucrat again. "You don't know?" He seemed amused—quietly so. "You really don't know?"

Max's hands went to her hips. "What don't I know?"

Bostock's upper lip curled, and his words dripped venomous contempt: "Anything. You . . . don't . . . know . . . *anything*."

"I'm crushed, Franklin," she said. "And here I thought you held me in such high regard."

The gun still trained on her, he shook his head. "You have no idea how important you are . . ."

"Now I'm *important*?"

". . . and you've just delivered yourself to me all tied up in a Christmas ribbon. But you are dangerous. Perhaps too dangerous to serve as a hostage . . ."

He pointed the gun at Max's head now, eyes tightening.

Alec and Joshua both started to rise, but Max patted the air, telling them to keep their position.

"If I'm so valuable, so important," she said, easing a half a step toward him, "why kill me?"

"Your death is inevitable—it's just a question of where and when . . . though it must be soon."

"I need to die . . . *soon*."

"Yes. You see, killing you represents victory, Max. May I call you 'Max'? 'Ms. Guevera' is too formal for us now, don't you think? . . . Your death means we win."

"You know, I always knew you snake-cult kids were a wacky bunch." She edged another few inches. "But maybe you can explain why the death of a mutant like me could be so important to a movement that dates back thousands and thousands of years . . ."

His laugh had a hint of hysteria in it. "You've really

never figured it out? . . . And Sandeman never *told* you?"

"Never met the guy. He was kind of a deadbeat dad, ya get right down to it." With each exchange now, she was narrowing the distance between them.

"A pity," Bostock said. "He might've had some fatherly advice for you. He might have told you to be more careful."

She squinted at him. "Am I in the same conversation? 'Cause I am definitely not following you, Franklin."

His arm straightened, the gun aimed squarely at her forehead. "You're going to die, that's a given . . . but considering all the grief you've given us, perhaps you do deserve to know just how badly you failed."

She moved another half step.

"That's far enough," he said, punctuating the sentence with a gesture of the pistol.

She halted. "*How* did I fail?"

He smiled, almost fondly. "Max, Max . . . you were the one . . . *the* one!"

"The . . . one."

"The *chosen* one, the new messiah!"

"Me. I'm Jesus."

"Yes. And how sad to die so close to one's birthday."

The guy was raving; even for a snake-cult practitioner, Bostock was 'round the bend. Max wasn't sure how much longer she could stall . . .

"Then maybe after you kill me," she said, "I'll be back in seven days . . ."

"I don't think so. This is a Christmas tale, Max . . . not Easter. So here's a gift: your 'father,' White's real

father, the fabled Sandeman, he got Manticore pulled
out from under him by a clandestine organization inside the government."

"That much I know."

Bostock went on as if she hadn't spoken. "But before he left, before Colonel Lydecker and the others
took over, he made one special child. You, Max."

"Well. Maybe my daddy *did* love me."

"In his way I'm sure he did. He did something very
special for you, Max—he spared you any junk
DNA . . . You're the only person—ordinary or transgenic or even Familiar—on this entire planet who is
like that. Even all the other Manticore freaks, like
pretty boy here, and Jo Jo the dog-face boy . . . they
have *some* flawed DNA. But not yours."

"And this makes me the Messiah how?"

Bostock frowned at her, as if he was dealing with
an imbecile. "You *still* don't see the bigger picture? A
pity Sandeman didn't put a few more grains of IQ
into that test tube."

She just looked at him. With a Christmas fruitcake
like this, what was there to say?

Bostock, his voice hushed, asked, "Do you know
about the Coming?"

Oh boy.

". . . The Coming?" she said. "Y'know, considering
I'm the Messiah and all, you'd think I would . . . but
why don't you fill me in."

Bostock's eyes showed white all around. "The
Coming is the end for most . . . but the beginning for
our people. Thousands of years of breeding have gone
into preparing us for survival from the Coming."

"You still haven't told me what the Coming *is*."

He raised his chin and the eyes had a wild cast. "When the comet comes, it will signify the end of the old . . . and the beginning of a brand new world."

Ames White's words echoed in her mind: *I want Ray to wake up Christmas morning in a brand new world.*

"This comet," Max said, "when . . ."

Bostock gestured to the ceiling . . . the sky . . . with his free hand. "It's visible once every 2021 years— that means this year. The last time was—"

Abruptly, Alec entered the conversation: "The Christmas star of Bethlehem . . ."

Bostock bowed, just a little. "Very good, young man."

Max swallowed. "And, uh . . . how exactly do I become the new messiah, out of a comet passing over the planet . . . two thousand years after the last messiah was born?"

He held the pistol steady on her, his gaze as steady as it was crazed. "Hard for me to believe you've had no signs . . . that Sandeman didn't find a way to tell you."

The markings!

Over the last year, runes that had started popping up on her flesh—new, instant tattoos unwantedly decorating her body, markings Logan had tried to translate, with no luck.

Bostock was wrong—Sandeman *had* found a way to let her know! She just hadn't figured it out, till this moment . . .

"With the coming of the comet," Bostock was saying, in a hushed voice worthy of church, "there will be a release of a biotoxin. It will wipe out the ordinaries—all those too weak to fight, too weak to be part of the new, pure order."

No need to stall him, she thought. Bostock was a zealot—he loved the sound of his own voice expressing the "sacred" beliefs of his cult.

"Only luck has prevented the catastrophe from repeating itself," he went on, using the bully pulpit that was the gun in his hand. "The comet is on an elliptical orbit that has brought it close enough for the biotoxin to reach Earth only once before—what do you think wiped out the dinosaurs? That time around, the ice age destroyed the toxin."

Max asked, "And this time around?"

"Christmas Eve—midnight, when the twenty-fourth becomes the twenty-fifth . . . that will be the next time the comet passes this close to the planet."

Alec said, "Close enough to drop off the biotoxin."

"Yes," Bostock said. "Death to the dinosaurs that walk the earth today—the ordinaries. The weak. Life to the Familiars. The strong."

Alec asked, "Which makes Max the Messiah how?"

"She is the only person on Earth completely immune to the virus."

Max said, "Because of Sandeman."

"Yes," Bostock said. "Even those of us with our special breeding face a small risk, as do the transgenics, but all of us—Familiars and test-tube mutants alike—should emerge unscathed. You, on the other hand, Max—there's no 'should' about it."

She arched an eyebrow. "Because I'm the 'Messiah'?"

"Because your unique DNA assures you that you will suffer no side-effects, no illness. Sandeman found a way to defeat the toxin, using frozen samples recovered from the polar ice cap. Your blood offers the ordinaries the same sort of vaccine potential that we have obtained through thousands of years of selective breeding."

"My blood," she said, not knowing whether to laugh or cry or do Daffy Ducks around the room, "could save the world?"

Bostock nodded, as if what she'd said was eminently reasonable. "Those ordinaries who don't die immediately upon exposure to the biotoxin might overcome it, given a vaccine developed from your blood. But when I kill you, Max, that possibility evaporates—the dream ends for humanity, and ours succeeds."

She held her palms out. "Sure you don't wanna drag me back to Snake Cult Central, and be the big man, for bagging lady Jesus?"

"It's tempting," he said with a tiny smile. "But you're a gifted young woman . . . and making the journey with you might be too great a risk."

Bostock's finger was poised on the trigger, and starting to squeeze.

Behind the Familiar, a window shattered . . .

. . . and Mole flew through, rolling once and popping up next to the stunned secretary; the pistol Mole had lifted from the Gulliver house was now scant inches from Bostock's skull, minus the silencer. They all stood frozen for a second, then Bostock, realizing the futility of his position, dropped his gun.

"What the hell took you so long?" Max asked Mole. "If this crazy son of a bitch wasn't so chatty, I might be dead by now!"

Mole had a big fat half-smoked cigar in his teeth, which had survived the trip through the window. He said, "I was listenin' on the ledge—entertaining BS, too. Anyway, you were about to jump his shit, weren't ya?"

That was true, but Max said, "Where the hell did you get the cigar?"

Mole shrugged. "Found a box of Havanas in Snake Boy's office downstairs."

"You took time to look for *cigars*?"

"Chill, Miz Messiah—Popeye needs his spinach, Mole needs his smokes."

If the lizard man hadn't just saved their skins, she might have been tempted to whale on him.

Puffing happily on his Havana, Mole jabbed the pistol into Bostock's ribs and said, "Sounds like Nixon here knows where Logan is."

Bostock stood silently, sullenly. He didn't seem particularly afraid, which bothered Max.

Mole got right on that, raising the pistol from the man's ribs to six inches from his left eye, thumbing the hammer back.

The tip of his stogie waggling an inch from his captive's cheek, Mole said, "Your problem, Bosty ol' boy, is it's Max here who thinks the sun rises and sets on Logan Cale. To me, he's just another annoying ordinary, which I'm sure you can identify with."

Sweat began to pearl Bostock's upper lip.

Mole went on: "Of course, I ain't crazy about you, either—though I do appreciate the Havanas. Even so, I'd just as soon pop one in your eye as not. So, asshole—you ready to die for the Conclave?"

Joshua finally entered the conversation, growling, "Take one for the team."

Bostock remained stoic.

Mole turned an eye toward Max.

"Screw it," she said. "When White calls next, we'll tell him everything and gamble he'll play ball."

Bostock said, "White will never—"

Max said to Mole, "Shoot him."

The secretary's eyes widened and his hands shot up, palms outstretched in front of him, pushing the air in a "be reasonable" fashion.

"Wait!" Bostock blurted. "Wait—I do know where Logan is . . . I can show you the way."

Mole eased the gun back a few inches.

Max came over to the pair then, her face less than a foot from Bostock's. "Selective breeding, and you're what they came up with?" She got out her cell phone, punched some buttons.

The voice in her ear was reassuringly sassy: "Original Cindy. Whatchu want?"

"It's me, Cin."

And Max outlined the situation for her friend.

"So," O.C. said, the sounds of Jam Pony in the background, "all I gotta do is rent a boat, drive it out to some godforsaken island in the middle of nowhere and babysit some old coot who's a vegetable?"

"That's all, Boo."

"No problem. But you gonna owe me, girl."

"As usual. And I need you to hook up with some-body else."

She gave Cindy the number of Sam Carr. Max was confident that once again Logan's doctor would make a house call.

"And tell Sam to bring Bling and/or other support. Couple guys who can handle themselves and are Eyes Only friendly."

"Hostile territory?"

"Yes—secured hostile territory, but hostile."

They searched the mansion one more time, making sure all of the security force was out of action; the survivors were rounded up and locked away in the basement. Then the little commando squad took a few minutes to grab some food—for now and later—in the Cale mansion kitchen.

But they couldn't afford to wait around for their friends to arrive and take charge of Lyman Cale. Max was confident Original Cindy could handle the situa-tion, and the X5 would check in with O.C. and Sam Carr by cell phone.

They took the boat back, got the car, and—follow-ing directions supplied by a suspiciously cooperative Bostock—hit the road.

"How do we know this button-down bastard ain't leadin' us on a wild goose chase?" Mole asked Max as he guided Logan's wheels down a back country road.

Hands and feet bound by duct tape, Bostock chuck-led in the backseat, jammed between Joshua and

Alec, who had the pistol pressed into the private secretary's ribs.

"You're easily amused," Max said to their prisoner.

Shaking his head, Bostock said, "I'm not leading you on a 'wild goose chase.' Not at all—I'm taking you right where you want to go."

"Yeah," Max smirked. "You're a great guy, Bostock. Class act."

He grunted a laugh. "You think you've won. You're only making my own inevitable victory that much easier. By hand-delivering you to the Conclave alive, I will not only shame White and his family, I . . . *I* . . . will become the chosen one. Ames White's defeat will be complete, as will my ascension."

"Sorry, Franklin," Max said, "but there's only room for one messiah in this car, and according to you, I'm it."

Everybody but Bostock laughed. Even Joshua got the joke.

"When we crucify you," Bostock said nastily, "you won't be coming back."

"Pretty cocky," Max said, "for a man on his way to see the father of the child he had murdered . . . Boy's body is in the trunk, by the way."

Bostock's smug facade faltered, but only for a moment. "White must be even softer than I thought if he lost to the likes of you."

Alec jammed the gun in the man's side. "Yeah," Alec said. "Takes a real schmuck to let transies like us get the better of him."

Her cell phone chirped. "Go for Max."

"It's Sam, Max. I'm with Lyman Cale."

"Can you do anything for him, Doc?"

"I'm arranging to have him taken out of here by private medivac—but I don't hold out much hope. The man has been nearly starved to death."

"These the medivac people Logan has used?"

"Strictly Eyes Only ops. Bling's with me now. We need to not hang around here, you know—you left some . . . trash."

The mansion and the grounds were littered with dead security guards. And of course a few live ones were salted away in the basement, and might get frisky, over time . . .

"You're right, Sam. Get out of there, ASAP. Get Logan's uncle some help, and you and Cindy to safety."

"Got it. Good luck. Stay safe."

"You, too, Sam. 'Bye."

She broke the connection.

"Dr. Carr?" Alec asked.

"Yeah. If Mr. Cale lives to see the New Year, it'll be a miracle." She turned to Bostock in the backseat, her voice icy. "By the way, if White doesn't kill you, I'm going to." Their eyes met for a long moment, and he kept his face impassive and proud; then she turned back—and heard a little gulp behind her.

They drove for hours and, as midnight passed and the temperature turned cold, Max wondered what exactly she and her friends could do to stop a comet that was supposed to wipe out mankind come Christmas.

The weirdest part was that she cared. Most of the ordinaries had shared nothing but revulsion and fear with her and her kind. If she was their damn messiah—and she'd had a sort of virgin birth, hadn't she?—she couldn't say she was wild about the idea of dying for their sins.

"That's it!" Bostock said from the backseat. "Just up ahead!"

Mole slowed.

At the mouth of a blacktop lane that cut through dense trees was a large white sign that said in bold black letters:

PRIVATE
NO ADMITTANCE
NO TRESPASSING
STRICT ENFORCEMENT

"Somebody doesn't have the Christmas spirit," Mole growled.

"That's the only way in," Bostock said, an excited edge in his voice.

"And out," Max said. She turned and looked at their captive, pointedly. "You'd just love us to go driving down there—a gate? A guard?"

Bostock was smiling. "Don't worry—when they find out it's you, the welcome will be warm."

Max's eyes went to Mole, who was shifting his latest stogie from one corner of his mouth to another.

"I don't think so," she said. "Keep driving."

Mole kept driving.

Both he and Max had a good sense of direction, a Manticore-tuned grasp of geography, and after a while she nodded to the lizard-man chauffeur to turn right onto a dirt road, which was little more than a path. It wasn't wide and didn't look like it had been traveled on for a good long time.

Still, something about the road had set off Max's radar, and she pointed to a grove of trees off to the left. "Pull in over there and park it. Kill the lights."

Mole eased the car off the road, onto the grass, and let it glide under the cover of the trees.

They all got out, Alec still holding the gun on Bostock, the bound secretary hopping along awkwardly.

"You're wasting your time," Bostock said.

"Gag him," Max ordered.

Joshua held Bostock while Alec went back to the car; soon Alec returned to give Bostock half a smile before jamming a rag in his mouth and circling his head with duct tape.

"I'm going up ahead to have a look," Max said. "Hang here—if I'm not back in half an hour, bail."

"I'll just tag along," Mole said.

"No. Stay with the group."

Joshua raised his hand like a school kid wanting to be excused, and said, "Me, then."

She shook her head. "It's just a recon—better off alone. I'll be back soon."

Before they could put up any more fuss, she took off.

She traveled less than a mile through the silent, dark woods, the evening chill making the temperature crisp again. The trees were close together, the grass not too tall, and above her, small meteors streaked across the sky, giving her a sense of foreboding.

She'd read in that rag Sketchy wrote for about the end-of-the-world comet, but hadn't taken it any more seriously than the vampire bat boy story or "Bigfoot Had my Baby."

But the comet *was* coming . . .

Still in the woods, she reached the top of a short hill and peeked around a tree to see what lay beyond.

Down the other side, past another patch of trees—alone in the middle of a wide, well-trimmed, sparse landscape—sat a three-story white stucco building and two outbuildings. Even from this distance she could see that bars covered the windows, and something C. J. Sandeman, the nutty brother of Ames White and evidently her half brother, had told her—when was it, a year ago?—came back to her.

"I'm not going back to their loony bin," C.J. had said.

From here the building indeed looked exactly like a no frills mental hospital. Below her, she knew, sat the stronghold of the Conclave.

Logan was in there somewhere—White, too; and God only knew how many Familiars, and what horrors . . .

But they had to go in. If they were walking into a trap, so be it; at least she'd be near Logan one last time.

The people in that bare-looking building—whether directly or indirectly—had been screwing with her since before she was born. It was too close to sunup to do anything now; they would sit tight during the day, and then tomorrow night it would be time to take the asylum away from those madmen.

Chapter Ten
SHOWDOWN AT BIG SKY

They took turns watching the Conclave stronghold from Max's spot atop the hill, facing the northwest rear corner of the building complex. Max had scouted all the way around the place, and this seemed to be the best, most easily defensible vantage point.

Though they couldn't see the front entry, they could monitor the parking lot and most of the compound; the lot had a dozen cars, plus a couple company vans, which was promising—it indicated the size of the staff, which would seem manageable, though she wouldn't have minded knowing if these Familiars were car-pooling.

Her foray around the far side of the building had provided little more than knowing that the sign out front identified this as BIG SKY RETREAT. When C.J. called the place a "loony bin," Max had no idea he was being this literal.

On the other hand, it made perfect sense for the Conclave's purposes: an ideal front, and a wonderful cover for both their sub-rosa activities and the keeping of any prisoners . . . Should any state inspectors come 'round, the only protestations they might hear would be courtesy of the inmates.

Of course, with the snake cult in charge, the lunatics really were running the asylum.

By dawn, Max and her minicommando squad had a pretty good idea of the Conclave's movements around the facility. Roving patrols of three took circuitous and seemingly random routes around the edges of the valley, into the woods surrounding the grounds of Big Sky; however, none of them came as far into the woods as the hill.

By Mole's count there had to be at least a dozen Familiars serving on patrol duty alone.

The four of them, up against an unknown number of selectively bred soldiers whose chief hobby in life was to wipe out transgenics—and Max was the snake-cult poster child of all transgenics, the "Messiah" the Conclave must smite.

Yow.

Funny thing was, troubled though she might be by the prospect of the apparently lopsided battle ahead, she didn't feel particularly frightened. They had faced long odds before and accomplished their missions; Manticore had instilled that ability, that attitude, within them.

But being up against an army so close to being their equals, and being decidedly outnumbered, did give her pause. This would definitely take a plan that didn't suck. They would need not only a solid scheme, but a diversion that would allow her to get Logan out.

She sat next to the car. Bostock, trussed up in duct tape, lay on the ground next to her, Alec sitting Indian-style, loosely training the pistol on their prisoner. Joshua was taking his turn at the watch post, and Mole was reclined in the front seat, catching z's before the fun.

"Cooperate with us," Max said to the gagged Familiar, "and I might help you stay alive."

He stared at her defiantly—or at least that was what she figured he was trying to do; mouth duct-taped like that, it wasn't really clear.

"You give me a rundown on the inside of that joint," Max said, "let me know how many of your fellow Snake Scouts of America are in there . . . I'll help you survive this. Interested?"

Still gagged, Bostock wriggled—like a snake, actually—and said something loud and angry, two words, the first one guttural, the second a vowel sound.

"I'm gonna take that for a no," Max said.

She walked over to a tree and withdrew her cell phone and punched in Dix's number, back at Terminal City. She got him on the first ring, and he was excited—relieved and worried—to hear her voice.

Max settled him down and filled him in, telling him where they were and what she had in mind.

"When?" he asked.

"Around midnight," Max said, and gave him more details. "Can you make it happen?"

"If we book," he said.

"Why don't you, then?"

"Roger that."

And Dix broke the connection.

For the rest of the day, they maintained their watch. A small basket of cold cuts and canned soda, brought along from the Cale mansion, provided sustenance— a rather grisly picnic, considering the basket had ridden in the trunk with the two corpses. The Manticore-trained soldiers weren't bothered by such trivialities, though, and an eerie calm touched their hilltop camp.

Alec, returning from his rotation, came up to Max and said, "You better take a look."

She joined him from their vantage point and saw a car rolling into the parking lot from that private lane—a black stretch Lincoln. The parking lot was now brimming with vehicles of many varieties— mostly expensive numbers, but not all.

"I make out license plates from all over the West Coast," Alec said. "Also, rental vehicles. What do you make of that?"

Max lowered the binoculars. "We're gonna have a full house of Familiars tonight. Comin' from miles around . . ."

"Why?"

She gave the X5 half a smile. "Big night for 'em."

"You mean, it's the annual snake-cult Christmas party?"

"No—it's the End of the World Fling. Comet's comin', remember?"

"Oh yeah . . . and, the good news is, Jesus is comin' back, right?"

She nodded. "Only they don't know the bad news: she's pissed."

Alec grinned and nodded. Then he looked at the sky. "I think we might have a white Christmas."

"Let's hope not much of one."

Around dusk a dusting of snow did arrive, but nothing troublesome; and then, after the dark came, its charcoal hand caressing the compound, they made their preparations for the coming battle.

They would have only one chance to free Logan—and it vexed Max that the fate of the man she loved depended largely on the whim of Ames White. But—though nothing was said, not directly—all of them knew that more than Logan Cale's future was at stake tonight.

For the cultists below, midnight marked a new future for their own twisted kind, and the beginning of the end for mankind. Whether there was any truth to it, Max couldn't say—what the hell could she do about a comet? On the other hand, the sick bastards below, who longed for the death of all ordinaries, and prayed for the death of transgenics, particularly herself, represented the kind of problem Max and her boys were eminently qualified to correct.

The transgenics had been bred to be soldiers to protect the United States from enemies foreign and domestic, and tonight, on homeland soil, they were finally going to get the opportunity to put those skills to use for their own country . . . at an insane asylum.

She watched them prepare now, her offbeat commando squad—Alec casually doing push-ups to burn off excess energy and stay limber; Mole checking the clip from his pistol (the presence of the weapon still troubled her); Joshua sitting on the ground, back to the car, legs straight out in front of him, his mouth yawned open in a silent roar as he slept.

Funny. They had come so far, the transgenics at Terminal City—their hometown finally accepting them, Alec about to run for city council, the arts and crafts mall revealing an entrepreneurial spirit, and a surprising well of creativity from within creatures trained to fight and to kill. They had come so far . . .

. . . and they had come far, making it to this hilltop, too. To fight. And to kill.

About ten minutes before midnight on Christmas Eve, Max stood with her three friends at the edge of the hilltop. The other messiah had three wise men to attend his birth: she had two wiseasses and a not so cowardly lion. Well, she'd take what she could get.

Nearby were the two corpses—the dead Familiar, rigid with rigor mortis; and the boy wrapped in the white sheet. She spoke to Mole and Joshua, telling them that when they reached the edge of the woods, they were to wait for her signal before emerging with their grim cargo. They nodded somberly.

Then she went up to Alec, who was tending to Bostock, keeping the gun snugged in the man's side. The private secretary still had not only his mouth but his arms and ankles duct-taped.

"Ready?" she asked Alec.

"Ready," Alec said. "But Max . . . before we do this . . ."

"Second thoughts? Like maybe you'd hate to see your political career nipped in the bud?"

"No. I have no second thoughts about helping take these sons of bitches down . . . but Max—consider."

He gestured with his head to the trussed-up Familiar. "If this guy is right . . . if these snake cultists are correct about this heavenly biotoxin . . . your blood is where the vaccine would come from, that would . . . you know."

"Save the world?"

"Something like that. Are you sure you're the person who ought to be walking up to the front gates of Snake City, ready to pick a fight?"

She didn't say anything for a moment.

Then she put a hand on Alec's shoulder. "I have considered that. But we're here to save Logan. I'm not prepared to believe anything these wackos say . . . but just in case, I'm putting you in charge of gettin' my carcass on ice, toot sweet."

He grinned at her. "Sure you wanna hand me a money-making opportunity like that?"

And she had to laugh. It felt good.

Then the two X5s exchanged serious nods, and Alec said, "Let's go wish those serpents a Merry Christmas, what do you say?"

"And help 'em shed their skins for the New Year," she said, and they bumped fists and started down the wooded hillside.

Max was in the lead, with Alec several paces behind her, guiding Bostock, who had to sort of hop along, else be dragged bodily by Alec. Joshua and Mole, carrying the corpses, were several paces behind Alec. Max's point position allowed her to spot one of the three-man patrols, in camouflage TAC apparel.

Bostock made some noise, and Alec slapped him with the pistol.

But Max was already on the move, throwing a kick into the lead guard. Suddenly Joshua and Mole—having laid down their gruesome burdens—were right there with her. A martial-arts blow to the neck from Max cancelled her guard's contract with life, and Joshua broke his guard's neck with a quick twist of both hands. Mole buried his gun so deep in his man's body that the guard's flesh muffled the shot.

Max looked over at Mole, the gun in his hand as he stood over the dead Familiar. He returned her gaze and whispered, "I know you don't like firearms, Max . . . but I gotta do this my way—'kay?"

Hating it, she nodded. Some part of her mind wondered how she could be such a hypocrite—after all, she'd crushed her opponent's windpipe with a knife-blade of a hand, the "gentle" giant Joshua had just snapped a Familiar's neck like a twig . . . and she was having trouble with Mole killing a man with a gun?

Maybe she could talk to somebody at Big Sky about this psychological hang-up of hers . . .

They were still fifty yards from the building when her cell phone rang.

"Go for Max."

"*Time's dwindling, 452,*" Ames White said, in the same distant, processed sound as his previous calls, as if he were on the moon and not, most likely, within shouting distance. "*Do you have my son?*"

"Yeah," she said. "He's here with me."

"*Put him on*"

"Not possible. We have to talk about that . . ."

"... *I'm getting the feeling I'm not going to like where this is going.*"

"Are you at Big Sky?"

Perhaps the question took him by surprise, as there was a long silence; she could almost hear the wheels turning, as her longtime antagonist tried to figure out just how much she knew.

"Yes or no?" she asked finally.

"*... Yes.*"

"Are you on a secure line?"

"*What do you mean, 452?*"

"I mean, are we 'alone' or are your friends listening in?"

"*I'm on my cell,*" he said, the tone implying he could talk.

"We've been enemies for a long time, White."

"*We agree on that much.*"

"But you need to know something ... We have mutual enemies."

Another pause.

Then: "*Where is my son?*"

"If you really are at Big Sky, step outside the front door and we'll talk about it. And White? Bring Logan."

She knew he'd be running to a window to try to see if she was serious. They were still behind the building, so there was no chance of White actually catching sight of them as they made their way through the trees toward the front.

"And don't bother contacting your foot patrol," she said, "to come up behind us. They're busy being dead."

White's voice took on an icy note. "*You always did know how to make an entrance, 452 . . . I'll be right out.*"

"Don't forget what I said, White—about mutual enemies."

"*How could I?*"

"Bring Logan."

"*I will. We have an exchange to make, right, 452?*"

"Right."

She clicked off.

Only a few stars dotted the night sky and a heavy chill hung in the air. Mole and Joshua, their arms filled with the dead, waited at the border of the woods as Max, Alec, and their duct-taped captive moved into the clearing, their feet crunching on the snow-powdered ground.

Floodlights on the corners threw pools of light around the building, spotlights awaiting a star performance; but Max and her company avoided them, stopping at the edge of an arc of light that shone from a floodlight above the main entrance.

She looked behind her, toward the trees; she could barely make out Mole and Joshua there, though the white of the boy's bedsheet shroud finally guided her to them. She gave a hand signal—*stay put*—and then nodded at Alec. He nodded back. Bostock, his ear a little bloody from where Alec had disciplined him, held his head up. He seemed to think he was about to turn from hostage to hero.

Max doubted that.

Then she, Alec, and the duct-taped prisoner moved into the pool of light.

The main entrance—double steel doors with wire-mesh-and-glass panels—was at the top of five concrete stairs lined with metal rails. The new masters of the world had selected unprepossessing main headquarters, to say the least. The trio faced the entrance in a loose line, Alec holding Bostock by the scruff of the neck, to her left; Max standing with her hands on her hips, defiant to the last.

The doors flew open and White—in a black suit and a thin black raincoat—stormed out. He stopped at the edge of the top stair, his eyes going to Bostock. He had changed not at all since she'd seen him last—his spiky dark hair looked frozen in place, his face ghostly pale under the floodlight, and his lips seemed to have no color at all, his dark eyes intense, burning.

Alone, he came down the steps, moving within fifteen feet of her.

"My son!" he yelled. "Where is he?"

Voices traveled clearly in the chill night air.

"I don't see Logan," Max said.

The doors erupted open and two dozen or more Familiars streamed out of the building and down the steps, in flowing reddish-copper hooded robes, monklike, the wind catching the garments. Some wore round metal collars engraved with pagan motifs; others had decorated their faces with black war paint; a few others had tattooed faces, reminiscent of heathen cultures from far-flung Pacific islands. Many, though, were bare of face—cultists who had infiltrated the world of the ordinaries . . . as Ames White had done, with the NSA. They filled in behind White, in a wide arc, a wind-shimmering wall of copper-red.

"Okay," Alec whispered to her. "We're officially outnumbered . . ."

One Familiar stepped up to White's side, immediately to his right—a tall wraith of a man with angular features and a hawkish nose, his hood back, exposing flowing silver hair; he wore neither markings nor tattoos. His regal bearing combined with the long robe—which included a scarlet tippet—gave him the appearance of a cleric or even a wizard.

Max had never seen this one before, yet his distinctive presence told her that he was their leader—that this was the Familiar who wielded the power.

At least, here at the nuthouse.

"Franklin," White said, acknowledging Bostock.

Behind his gag, Bostock said something unintelligible.

"Where," Max asked, "is Logan?"

White's head tilted. "Where's Ray?"

She gestured with open hands. "Look—you've got us outnumbered. We're on your home field. Give us what we came for—how are we gonna get away before you get want you want?"

White considered that, then gave a quick nod.

"Bring him!" the silver-haired Familiar called.

Two more hooded, robed figures burst through the doors, one on either side of Logan Cale, who they dragged down the stairs.

The crowd parted and the Familiars hauled Logan up by either arm; he wasn't bound, but seemed weak, even groggy. They stopped on White's left, maintaining their hold on him.

Logan's eyes met hers.

"Surprising," he said, "the lengths I'll go to, Max, to get back on your good side."

For a guy who'd been the guest of Ames White and the snake cult, he didn't look so bad—they hadn't let him shave, and the beard gave him a scruffy cast; his clothes—jeans, pullover blue sweater—were filthy and wrinkled. But there were no obvious signs that he'd been beaten or tortured, and—despite the Familiar at either arm—he was standing on his own two feet; they obviously had not deprived him of the exoskeleton that allowed him upright mobility.

She smiled at him and said, "You're not forgiven yet."

He grinned and shrugged, and she grinned and shrugged.

"All very brave and touching," White said, and he withdrew a Glock from under the raincoat, "but if he speaks again before I have my boy, I'll kill him."

Max held her palms out and up. "White, I need you not to do anything rash . . ."

"*Where* is *Ray?*"

"You need to *listen*. You have the advantage here. Wait until you've heard it *all*."

White's frown revealed an inner battle between rage and curiosity, impatience and willpower. "Heard *what*, 452?"

Max raised her hand, issued signals, lowered her hand.

"Nothing rash," she advised him.

White's frown deepened.

Mole and Joshua emerged from the shadows, their arms filled with the terrible cargo; it was as if they were two somber grooms carrying brides over the threshold. Mole put the dead Familiar on the ground in front of the silver-haired leader. Joshua put the smaller, sheet-wrapped body down before the boy's father.

Ames White did not have to lift the sheet to know— the small form said it all. In a voice that he was obviously straining to keep emotion-free, White said, "Ray."

"Yes," Max said. "But I didn't do this."

The gun in White's hand swung up and he leveled the barrel at Logan's temple. White's lips were peeled back over his teeth in a skull's smile, and Logan winced . . .

"My people did not do this terrible thing!" Max screamed. "Or don't you really care who *did* do it!"

White remained poised there, ready to shoot, for several long moments. Then the gun came down, his eyes narrowed, and he turned his homicidal gaze on Max.

"If you didn't, 452," he said, "who did?"

"Ask *him*!" Max said, and pointed at Bostock.

Alec ripped the duct tape from the man's face. Bostock spat the rest of the gag, the knot of cloth, onto the snowy ground.

White said, "Do you have something to say, Franklin?"

Bostock stood frozen.

Max said, "He was talkative before. Maybe he's a little intimidated in the presence of the father of the child he ordered killed."

"Explain," White said.

The silver-haired leader gripped White's arm and whispered in his ear. But White shook his head and yanked his arm away.

"*Explain!*"

Max quickly told White that she'd first encountered Bostock trying to get ransom aid from Lyman Cale.

"That makes sense," White said, astonishingly self-composed, but not looking down at the little sheet-wrapped corpse. "Approaching Lyman Cale for the ransom . . . but how did you recognize Franklin as a Familiar?"

She explained tracking Ray down. "When we got to the house, we were too late, only by moments, but too late—two men had executed Ray and his aunt. One got away, but we stopped this one . . ."

She gestured to the dead Familiar in the snow.

She went on: "I recognized him as one of the security guards employed by Bostock."

Mole stepped forward and flipped the corpse over, giving White a good look at the face of the Familiar.

Almost gently, she asked, "Recognize him?"

White nodded.

Max said, "He was assigned to Lyman Cale, wasn't he?"

White nodded, his gaze on the secretary now.

"We're enemies, White," Max said. "But I wouldn't have killed your boy. For one thing, I needed him, to get Logan back. For another, I'm not a sick son of a bitch, like Franklin, here."

The secretary tried to break away from Alec, but the X5 grabbed him by the arm and shoved the gun back in his ribs.

"What do *you* have to say, Franklin?" White asked, in a tone that was all too reasonable.

Bostock said nothing.

"Is it true, Franklin? Did you kill my son? Why would you do such a thing . . . to a Brother?"

Ignoring White, Bostock turned toward the tall, silver-haired monklike figure. "Matthias! You know I would do anything to further the goals of the Conclave—*anything!* And White, here . . . he's failed so many times. Open your eyes, Matthias! Look who I have delivered unto you! How many times has White failed, and who is it that brings her to you—the One!"

Disturbingly, White was smiling, his arms folded, the gun casual in his grasp. The robed figure—Matthias—listened to Bostock's pleas impassively, his expression blankly unreadable.

Bostock was saying, "And when she's gone, there will be nothing that can stop the Conclave's directives from being carried out. I brought her to you—on this, the night of nights!"

Bostock's voice echoed across the grounds.

"The Coming," he was saying, "is but minutes away—we are close to final victory, total victory . . . *because of me.* I brought her to you! Not White. Not this . . . spawn of Sandeman, the father of all of our problems."

Still, Matthias said nothing—his eyes bright, as he stared at Bostock. A hint of approval . . . ? Max wondered.

Finally, the secretary said, "Yes, I had Ray White killed, another weak spawn of Sandeman—but it was part of my design, the plan to bring her to you . . . and here she stands. She is here. She is ours—*yours*. Kill her now, and the future is ours."

White glanced, almost casually, at the silver-haired man. Their eyes met for a brief instant, and Matthias—almost imperceptibly—nodded.

White raised his pistol and shot Bostock in the head.

Bostock went straight back, flopping onto the snowy ground, sending up puffs of white; the black hole in his forehead was ringed with red, and he lay looking at the sky with wide, empty eyes, as if even in death he was anticipating the arrival of the comet.

White brought his pistol to bear on Max. "The fool was right about one thing, 452—you do need to die."

"The comet!" someone in the crowd shouted, and others blurted the same. They milled, wide eyes raised, arms and hands upraised, a sea of faces salted with the ritual markings, some paint, some inked flesh.

White's eyes went to the sky, too, where a stream of sparks flew across, exploding in a shower of color.

The rocket provided the diversion Max needed—she would kiss that spudhead Dix the next time she saw him—and, as White realized the ruse of the fireworks and swung the gun back around, firing it at her, the shot sailed wide, Max diving toward the two Familiars holding Logan's arms. She flung one off, kicked the other in the head, and held her hand out to Logan.

He took it.

More rockets streaked across the sky, and not all of

the Familiars were wise yet, though several had taken time out from the display to attack Joshua, Alec, and Mole in a flurry of martial-arts moves, bizarrely awkward coming from the robed warriors, yet formidable. The snow-dusted grounds glowed yellow and orange under the momentary daylight.

"It's fireworks, you fools!" White yelled.

And then all of the Familiars were on them.

The quartet of transgenics fought hard, but it was clear that the Familiars' numbers were just too great. The only plus—other than White—was that the cultists did not seem to be armed; they had gathered at Big Sky to party, not fight.

Logan was slugging it out, too, but he was weak and no match for Familiars.

Then, echoing up through the woods, came battle cries.

Dix had brought more than just fireworks from home.

A hundred transgenics stormed out of the forest and joined in the fray—Dix and Luke and so many strange, familiar faces. A few brandished weapons, but mostly it was just a wave of sheer mutant force, sweeping onto the wintry landscape.

She stepped in and helped Logan, who was battling the two Familiars who'd held him captive before, and her kicks to the throat and groin and every other dirty tactic that could actually get through to a Familiar were enough to put the two down, at least long enough for her to grab Logan by the hand again and look him in the eyes and say, "*Run*—Logan, go to the woods and wait!"

He shook his head and went for another of the Familiars. She loved him for wanting to stay and stand to fight at her side, but it was a decision as stupid as it was brave. Within seconds he was on his back on the ground, the Familiar looming over him, choking the life out of him.

She head-butted a tattooed face in front of her, the man's nose exploding in a scarlet shower; he wobbled but did not fall, and it took an elbow in the throat to convince him to do so. She got behind the one strangling Logan, grabbed his head and gave it a good hard twist, snapping his neck. Before the dead weight could fall on him, Logan rolled out from under.

She knelt next to Logan, who was groggy, face red, from the near strangulation; a gunshot cracked the night and something hot erupted through her shoulder, knocking her back. She lay there, looking up at an enormous sky, seemingly filled with stars, but it was just Dix's fireworks display continuing to go off. Turning her head to the right, she saw Logan reaching out to her—he was dazed, his eyes wide in horror—and their hands touched and she felt peaceful, happy, a quiet settling over, banishing the battlefield . . .

. . . but the sensation lasted only a moment, as White jumped on top of her, straddling her, pulling her up to him by her vest. In a way, he did her a favor, snapping her back to full consciousness and a world much bigger than just her and Logan; again she was cognizant of the sounds of fighting around her, the explosions in the sky . . . and Ames White's tortured, demonic face inches from her own.

"Bostock may have killed Ray, 452," he said, and he was smiling though there was pain in it—Familiar or not, he was a father who'd suffered the greatest loss— "but you caused it, didn't you? Like every misfortune that's been rained down on me in the last year and a half—*you*."

He raised the barrel of his pistol toward her face to deliver the kill shot.

Lips peeled back over that terrible smile, he said, "My son won't live to rule . . . but I will. Your death at my hands assures me of that immortality."

She watched in seeming slow motion as his finger squeezed down on the trigger. She could almost see the bullet ready to ride the black tunnel from firing pin to her skull. In that instant a thousand thoughts coursed through her mind, all at once and yet each one clear, concise, easy to see.

The people who were important to her, the things that made her happy, what she would do with her life, her life with Logan Cale, if just somehow in the next second this bullet failed to blow her brains out . . .

Above the cacophony of the battle, she heard something primal and horrifying, and then a beast loomed above and behind Ames White . . .

Joshua.

The gun fell with a thunk next to her, and she heard the cry from White . . . Was it pain? He couldn't feel physical pain . . . could he? Was it rage, or sorrow, or just some gargling horrible sound that a man might make, should a beast grab him by the skull . . .

. . . and yank.

She did know that White's head disappeared from her view, and the weight of him lifted off her.

She was on her elbow, propping herself up, when she saw White—or anyway, White's body—on the ground next to her, red pumping out of the pipelike opening of his neck, a wide geysering spigot where his head had been.

And when Max sat up, she saw where that head was now—six and a half feet above her, where Joshua held the detached cranium, by the hair, at eye level, staring into White's lifeless face.

"You shouldn't have done it," Joshua said, and his voice was strangely gentle, scolding the blood-dripping head, as if warning a child. "You shouldn't have killed Annie."

Annie . . . the ordinary Joshua had loved, and who loved him, a gentle blind girl who White had slain out of sheer meanness.

Joshua was staring at White's head, as if waiting for an apology.

Then, when no apology came, a cry of anguish rose from deep within the leonine figure, and he swung his arm, like an airplane propeller, and cast the head into the dark night, where it landed with a distant plop.

Suddenly Joshua was leaning down over her, saying, "Sorry, Little Fella. Kinda lost my head."

She just looked at him, wondering if he knew what he'd said. Then Joshua was pulling her up to her feet, and she inspected her wound—the shoulder was stiff, but the bullet seemed to have gone on through, and her transgenic body was already working at repairing itself. Rolling the shoulder a little, she said, "Gonna be all right."

Joshua helped up Logan, too.

She quickly surveyed the battle—transgenics outnumbered Familiars now—looking for that silverhaired ghost, Matthias.

She spotted him, on the run, the long robe flowing behind him, the tippet flapping, as he headed up the stairs and back inside the asylum.

"Stay out here," she told Logan and Joshua, "till the building's secure . . . Alec! Mole! Follow me!"

Chapter Eleven
THE END

Max waded into the sea of robed Familiars. Behind her, in an impressive display of martial-arts prowess, Alec was handily dealing with a pair of the cultists. Mole was off to the one side, taking care of another of the armed three-man TAC patrols, blasting away at them mercilessly, and they fell like camouflaged bowling pins.

But soon the two warriors—in answer to her call—were at her back, as she plowed her way toward the steps to the front entry of the hospital.

The tide of the fight had turned decisively toward the transgenics. Those Familiars who weren't already lying in broken heaps on the ground were taking flight, a few literally heading for the hills, others around the building, presumably for another way inside or perhaps to make it to the parking lot—and, in either case, the ragtag transgenics gave chase.

Once they were up the short flight of steps, Max, Mole, and Alec went inside unimpeded. For all the frenetic and violent activity outside, the asylum itself seemed deserted. Initially, they found themselves in what had once been a reception/waiting room area, with a double-door elevator, but no chairs lined the walls, and the nurse/receptionist window was vacant; otherwise, it was just a big empty slab room, cut through the middle by a long hallway.

Though voices could be heard, the cries of prisoners, these did not emanate from this floor—in fact, they sounded more like they were coming from the walls. The effect was ghostly, troubling, but this floor was clearly administrative, small tidy offices with computers and desks and chairs and files, as you might find in any institution of this type. The thought of the inhabitants of these neat offices being cultists with pagan facial markings, parading in flowing hooded robes, chanting ritual gibberish, seemed utterly absurd . . . or would have, if they hadn't just pushed their way through a throng of them out on the battlefield that the asylum grounds had turned into.

The building was old and badly in need of renovation, yet the place was neat, floors dust-free, no cobwebs, the walls and ceilings clean, the entire facility smelling of pine cleaner and disinfectant.

Moving cautiously, Max signaled for them to split up, Alec and Mole each taking one of the side halls while Max went down the middle.

Max found fire stairs at the end and started up.

The second floor was cells—cries for help, shouts for attention, echoed down the hallways. No guards were around, no robed Familiars—no one home but the inmates. She had a good idea who they were:

prisoners of the Conclave, perhaps ordinaries who'd tipped to the evil practices and intentions of the Familiars, or betrayers among their own ranks, possibly even transgenics—mixed with the real mental patients who'd provided the cover.

On the third floor landing she found another small reception area, this one not so spare—nicely paneled, with comfortable chairs and magazines on end tables, another window (empty, of course) where a nurse and or receptionist could sit.

She pushed through double doors down a short corridor of examination rooms and more small tidy offices. The medicinal scent was strong, making her nose twitch, but that was well in keeping with what seemed a clinic of some kind. This section of the building seemed to her a facade designed to fool state inspectors and those families who really were committing their loved ones (unwittingly) to snake-cult care.

At the end of the short hall was a windowless metal door, with no knob—just a slot for an ID card. In bold red letters on the gray door it said:

NO ADMITTANCE

Well, surely *somebody* could go in there, she thought. What was the point of a place that no one could be admitted to?

So she kicked the door down. It was solid and took two tries, but on the second it went flying and clattered to an obsidian floor.

She got a quick look at the room—a large rounded

chamber, with a planetarium-type dome, a vast
curved viewing window that made the starry sky, in
effect, the room's ceiling. The circular room, dimly
lighted by recessed fixtures, was wall-to-wall stacked
monitors; a dozen seats—empty at the moment—
faced these monitors, with computer stations at each
post. About a third of the monitors were security
cams—showing inmates in their cells, views of the
grounds and hallways and stairs and the downstairs
reception area, and the area she'd just come through,
for that matter.

The rest of the monitors were satellite images from
all around the world, each boldly labeled with a red-
letter readout that identified the city shown, as well as
the local time—she glimpsed Chicago, New York,
Los Angeles, San Francisco, Miami, Seattle, Toronto,
Moscow, London, Lisbon, Sydney, and on and on. On
the screens were live pictures of the cities, in popu-
lous areas—Chicago's cam was on Michigan Avenue,
near the Water Tower, and New York was, of course,
Times Square, where Christmas Eve had turned into
something approaching New Year's Eve, people with
little glowing candles in hand, watching the sky, waiting for the comet to come.

And in the center of the room, raised up on a five-
foot platform, was a molded black chair, strangely
like a human hand rising to caress the person perched
there, with controls built into the wide flat armrests—
Captain Kirk's chair, revised by Salvadore Dali. In
this chair, this throne, his hood back, sat silver-haired
Matthias.

All of this she took in, in a moment, which was all

she had before a figure flew at her, snarling, a priestess with a ceremonial dagger in one hand and long clawed nails ready with the other. Rather lost in her robe, the priestess was slender and lovely, or would have been if her face had not been covered in ritual tattoos, and she took Max down in a diving roll, one powerful arm and hand slipping around Max as the knife rose.

But before the blade fell, Max grasped the arm hugging her and snapped it like a twig, then flung the woman off—the priestess, Familiar or not, was feather light.

One arm dangling, useless, the priestess hissed and came at Max low, charging, knife again raised; and Max sidestepped her, latching onto the flowing robes and running her headlong into one of the monitors, crashing the woman's head through the screen in a shower of glass and an eruption of smoke and flame.

"So much for monitoring London," Max said to Matthias as the priestess shuddered and shivered, literally jolted as electrocution won out over centuries of selective breeding.

Matthias swiveled toward Max. He seemed not at all concerned, certainly not a whit distraught over the loss of the priestess.

"In the pre-Pulse world," Matthias said to her, his voice rich, strangely soothing, with a faint Teutonic lilt, "such demonstrations of your mutant powers might impress. Now . . . as we await the momentary arrival of the Coming, seeing such a childish display on your part, 452 . . . seems almost nostalgic."

She kept her distance from him, for the moment;

his hands were on controls on those armrests, and she had no idea what he could do from his perch.

She heard something behind her, whirled, and it was Alec, with Mole bringing up the rear.

"Whoa," Alec said. "Dude's got *some* home entertainment center . . ." He nodded toward the slumped, smoking priestess hanging out of the London monitor. "But y'know, it's dangerous, if you sit too close to the screen."

Mole, glancing around, said, "So who's this character? Blofeld? . . . Building's clear of snake suckers, except for this guy. Lots of inmates, though, on the second floor."

Matthias seemed bored with them. But he granted them this observation: "The Coming is inevitable. Your efforts . . . They are small, pitiful attempts, small boats hoping to ride out a typhoon."

Hardly listening, Alec was staring at the ceiling. "Now, *that's* a skylight . . ."

Matthias gestured toward a bank of monitors—in the hooded, loose robe, it was like the specter of death, pointing.

"We flee into the night, and you cannot stop us," he said.

Among the monitors were views of the parking lot, where robed Familiars were frantically getting into their cars and booking.

"Where do you keep your car keys in those cloak things?" Alec asked.

Max shot him a look.

"Just wondering," Alec said.

"Some of our brothers have fallen tonight,"

Matthias said. "But these others will go out into the world and spread the word . . . and our seed . . . even as the ordinaries wither like unpicked fruit on the vine."

Alec, still chatty, asked, "So in a few minutes, when this biotoxin hits . . . How long's it take to kick in?"

"Many will die in moments," the silver-haired Familiar said. "Others, the strongest of a weak species, will cling to life."

"And Max here," Alec said, "can give 'em a clean bill of health, once we get the vaccine goin' . . . Mole, you're a businessman. How much do you think we can get, for a shot of Maxine?"

Max arched an eyebrow. "Maxine?"

"Vaccine . . . Max . . . get it? We'll have to trade-mark it."

Mole was not amused. "Let me ice this sucker, and let's be home for Christmas."

Matthias stood, looming over them. *"Kon'ta ress! Ken'dra hiff!"* He was staring at the sky—the stars—and, seemingly, speaking to them. His arms out-stretched. He continued the ancient incantation: *"Adara mos rekali . . . konoss rehu jek!"*

Mole, raising his pistol, said, "Nobody can make me listen to this crapola . . ."

"The future!" Matthias's voice echoed through the dark, dim chamber, the monitors glowing like small fires. "The future . . . arrives!"

The trio of transgenics followed the Familiar's fin-ger to the glass dome . . .

. . . and saw a streak of silver and gold, appearing in the sky, a fiery Christmas ribbon flung across the heavens, its tail a shimmering scattering of white sparks.

"Cool," Alec said.

Max had never seen anything quite so beautiful, nor so breathtaking. And still she shuddered: was that stardust trail the bearer of the biotoxin—the beginning of the end for mankind . . . ?

Matthias stood on his roost, his eyes going from one monitor to another . . .

On some of the screens, faces shone with delight from the sight of the Christmas comet. In some locales, a sea of small candles glowed, as if at a church service; in others, gay streamers of silver shook in upraised hands, in happy imitation of the remarkable event they'd just seen. Though there was no sound from the monitors, it was clear cheers and hoops and hollers and whoops of Yuletide joy were ringing in the air at the various locales. And then, slowly, spectators began to filter off, into their own lives, their own celebrations of the holiday . . .

. . . and they all looked just fine.

Matthias stared with an astounded expression— Max had never seen a longer puss on a guy. He kept shifting his vision from one monitor to another, and all he could see was ordinaries having a good time . . . clearly feeling hunky-dory.

"Maybe it takes a while to kick in," Alec said. He seemed vaguely disappointed. "An hour or so."

"Or maybe a thousand years," Max said.

Matthias sat—heavily—in his black chair; it was as if the hand shape of it was trying to crush him.

"Hey, don't be down in the dumps," Mole said,

stepping up to him. "Do what the other end-of-the-world cults do, when the big day craps out on 'em. Pick a new one! Revise and move on."

"We . . . are . . . superior," Matthias said, dazed.

"Sure you are," Max said. "I read about this cult . . . before the Pulse? A comet was coming to take them to outer space, where God was waiting for 'em. First the men had to castrate themselves . . ."

"Ouch," Alec said.

". . . and then take poison. Purify themselves—y'know, you don't want to meet God without sprucing up a bit. But they just *knew* that comet was gonna take 'em to outer space. Guess what? They're still waiting."

Matthias looked directly at Max, his expression haunted. "It was predetermined thousands of years ago. We *shall* prevail—"

"Maybe next comet," Alec said. "When's that, 4006?"

Max stepped nearer to Matthias. "Can you control the facility from where you sit?"

Matthias turned his gaze upon her. "Of course."

"Then unlock all the cells . . . Cooperate, and we'll spare you."

Mole said, "Hey! I say we—"

"It's not a democracy," she reminded him. Then to Matthias she said, "Well?"

Matthias's ice-blue eyes fell to the computer screen built into the armrest—he touched the screen, in a "button" at the upper right . . .

. . . and the monitors changed image.

All of them the same.

All, in huge red numbers, reading: *5:00*. For one second, that is; then they read: *4:59 . . . 4:58 . . . 4:57 . . .*

Max jumped onto the perch and grabbed him by the front of his robe. "What the hell—"

"This facility will self-destruct in five minutes. More or less. Less, now."

She put her hands on either side of his face and looked at him, as if she were going to kiss the silver-haired leader. "You won't have to wait," she said.

And broke his neck.

Hopping down, she said, "Alec—take a look at those controls. We got *minutes* to clear this place and get our people off these grounds!"

Mole pitched what was left of his latest stogie and grumbled, "Why can't these megalomaniac meat-heads be satisfied with killin' themselves? Why do they gotta take a bunch of people with 'em?"

"We'll break up into discussion groups later," Max said, unceremoniously pulling the corpse of Matthias by his feet down off the throne onto the black floor, while Alec scrambled up in his place.

She looked at him, hopeful. "Think you can unlock 'em?"

"No problem." Alec touched a button.

The explosion rocked the building and knocked Max on her butt.

She sat there, next to dead Matthias, and again looked up at Alec. Not so hopeful.

Alec gave her half a grin and half a shrug, and said, "I seem to have blown up one of the outbuildings."

Getting on her feet, she said, "Don't just go touching any more buttons, until you're sure, okay?"

Four thirty-four . . . 4:33 . . . 4:32 . . .

"Maybe I should crack open a brewski," Alec said, "and read the manual . . . You know, at my leisure?"

"Just do it, Alec," she said, and she and Mole were out of there.

Max told Mole, as they sprinted down the stairs, "You take the cells on the left, I'll take 'em on the right . . . If Alec can't unlock 'em, just pull the damn things off their hinges."

"No prob," Mole said.

That was when the sprinkler system started in, whether automatically—thanks to the explosion of the outbuilding, its fire presumably spreading—or by more experimentation on Alec's part, she had no idea. The indoor rain felt icy cold and smelled of rust, as though it had been captive in the asylum's pipes for a long time.

Max prayed that Alec had found the button to unlock these doors . . .

In the long bare hallway, she tugged on the first door and nothing happened. She cursed, but it was inaudible over the sound of the sprinklers and voices screaming in cells all along the hall.

Finding a fire extinguisher in a box on the wall, Max elbowed the glass, got the thing out and started clanging it against the lock of the first door. Finally, the old lock gave way and she threw open the door . . .

On the single bed suspended by chains from the wall, a wide-eyed C. J. Sandeman lay wrapped in a straitjacket and gagged. Even so, it was clear that he recognized her immediately.

"No time to get you outta that," she said, yanking him off the cot, steadying him onto his feet. "Building's going up in a couple minutes. Get down to the first floor, they'll help you."

He managed to nod and stumbled out and off toward the stairs.

Mole tried a door, looked at her bright-eyed. "This one's unlocked!"

Quickly he opened it and stuck his head in.

Just as quickly he yanked his head back out and slammed the door shut.

Mole shuddered.

"What?" she asked.

"Snakes," he said, and went on.

You'd think *he* wouldn't have a problem with that, she thought, going on to the next cell, trying to keep track of time. About two minutes left . . .

With the water coming down, her hair was well-matted by now. She had released four prisoners when she finally heard the locks all click open. All the doors thrummed open slightly and the prisoners needed no further encouragement than that. They flew down the hall, splashing, barely aware of Max waving them toward safety. She stayed on the floor, going from cell to cell making sure everyone got out.

She saw no other inmate or prisoner until she got to the last door, which she opened wide, and looked in to see a lump in the middle of a padded cell whose stuffing was largely hanging out of gaping tears.

"Get on your feet!" she said. "Building's gonna blow!"

The lump rolled over to reveal a sickly, emaciated man who had obviously undergone a great deal of torture, a man who stared at her with beady dark eyes . . .

. . . a man she had known all her life.

Stunned, all she could say was, "I thought you were dead."

Colonel Donald Lydecker—the dreaded surrogate father of all the Manticore siblings—looked up at her, his hands shakily reaching toward her. "Not if you help me . . ."

She recoiled. "Go to hell. Get out on your own, if you can, you bastard."

And she turned to go, the time pressing her harder than this stunning discovery.

But behind her a weak version of that strong voice called out over the sprinkler din: "I understand how you feel . . . but if you help me . . . I'll help you."

Her back to him as she stood poised in the door, she said, "Help me? Like you've helped me in the past, killing my sibs?"

She was halfway out when his words stopped her: "I know where your mother is."

Her birth mother . . . her father a test tube, but her mother a real woman, who Max had longed to find, to meet, to know . . .

As the clock ticked, her mind flew: he was lying; Lydecker always lied. He knew her hot buttons and had pushed the hottest one he could think of . . . that simple.

She left him there and went running down the hall.

And then she turned and sprinted back to duck into the cell and scoop up her sickly surrogate father.

The transgenics were scattered across the grounds, robed figures sprawled around them on the snow-dusted landscape. Among the dead, the white-sheeted body of the boy stood out, as did the headless corpse of his father. Here and there a few of the patrol guards, in TAC gear, lay dead, shot by Mole. Any way you figured it, the battle was over, the opponents either dead or badly injured . . . those who hadn't fled.

"Building's gonna blow," she cried, "any second! *Run!*"

And they ran.

It galled her that she was the one hauling Colonel Donald Lydecker to safety.

They were at the edge of the woods when the building exploded—actually, three small explosions placed around and within the building that together rolled up into one big one, and one fireball, flinging chunks of stone and showering debris like an ugly, landbound comet.

Within a very short time the fallen, half walls of the complex—though one outbuilding stood, relatively unscathed—were home to orange, licking flames and foul, rolling gray-black smoke, the crackling of the fire like sporadic gunfire.

And then the bearded Logan was at her side. He glanced down at the withered form of Lydecker, shivering, coughing, and said, "Look what the cat drug in."

"I wish I hadn't," she said, and told Logan what Lydecker had said.

"You can't trust him," he said.

"I know. I know."

"But Max . . . you can trust me. Really."

"I know, Logan."

"You do?"

"Going to your uncle for the ransom . . . he almost died, because of me, Logan. He may still die . . . he's comatose. And I knew . . . if I caused his death . . . telling you would be the hardest . . ."

He took her hand in his—flesh-to-flesh, no virus to worry about—and squeezed it. "You did this for me, Max. I know you did. You rid mankind of this demented snake cult . . . or anyway, diminished their ranks considerably, including Ames White himself . . . but you didn't do it for mankind, did you?"

"No. It was for you, Logan . . . We hadn't finished our argument."

He laughed, gently.

Alec had noticed Lydecker's disheveled presence, and said, "I can't believe this bastard's alive!"

"I can fix that," Mole said, brandishing the pistol.

She shook her head, made a sharp motion. "*No!* I need him, breathing."

The reptile face wrinkled further and words came through clenched teeth: "But it's what I want for Christmas."

Again Max shook her head. "I'll get you a tie."

"What about the comet?" Alec asked. "From what we saw on those monitors, people all over feel fine . . . Other than a hangover tomorrow, maybe. It was a big nothin'!"

Logan said, "Maybe it'll have effects on people like

me, in the days ahead . . . but I don't think so. The
snake cult may have been physically and mentally superior, thanks to all that 'good' breeding . . . but they
were still a cult. It was religion they were spouting—
not science."

"What if it does kick in?" Max asked.

Logan shrugged. "We do what people always do—
our best to survive, a day at a time."

"I coulda told you it was BS," Alec said.

Max looked at him. "Yeah?"

"Never believe *anything* in that rag Sketchy writes
for."

There was laughter—a relief after the hard-fought
struggle—and Max and Logan pitched in with first
aid, patching up some wounds among the transgenics,
including her own shoulder. Fortunately, the lack of
firearms and other weapons among the Familiars—
who'd not been prepared for an invasion tonight, mutant or otherwise—had limited casualties among the
ranks of the good guys.

The transgenics Dix had rounded up to play cavalry
for Max and her little crew had made the trek in various
vehicles—trucks, cars, vans, even schoolbuses, all of
them having two things in common: the vehicles were
old as dirt, and ran like new, thanks to the Terminal City
motor pool of Luke and Dix. Max said her good-byes,
giving Dix that big kiss he deserved, and she—and
Mole, Alec, Joshua, and Logan—waved as the unlikely
caravan of vehicles started home.

Mole returned to the compound, where the fire
was starting to die down, and commandeered a truck
from behind the one surviving outbuilding—neither

Matthias nor Alec had managed to blow that one up—and, soon, they were loading Lydecker in the back with the rest of them and heading out the front gate (the guard post abandoned) to drive around to where Logan's car waited, undisturbed.

Logan and Max climbed down out of the truck, and Max instructed Mole to take the vehicle back to Terminal City with Lydecker . . . alive.

"Call Dr. Carr and get him some medical help," she said to the lizard man. "And keep Lydecker under lock and key, and constant guard. When he gets to feeling better, he'll be slippery."

"You're putting me in charge?" Mole asked, lighting up a cigar.

"I know you'd just as soon rip his head off as look at him," Max said.

Mole glanced Joshua's way. "I don't know, Max—that kinda thing ain't exactly *my* department."

Joshua looked away, embarrassed.

Max thumped Mole's chest. "Just make sure that evil bastard stays alive. If he can help me find my mother, that's one good thing he can do, after all the bad."

"Starting a new crusade already?" Alec asked. "Can't we take a day or two off?"

"You know us messiahs," Max said. "We're savin' souls seven days a week."

"I thought you rested on Sunday," Alec said.

"No," Max said. "You're thinkin' of my Old Man."

Alec smirked. "Test tubes *never* sleep."

Then Terminal City's next alderman crawled in back of the truck, where Lydecker had been propped up, half out of it. Joshua, riding shotgun, waved like a little kid. Mole, behind the wheel, stogie in the corner of his mouth, winked at her.

And they disappeared into the bright morning.

Christmas morning.

The couple got into Logan's car, Max behind the wheel.

"So I'm forgiven?" Logan asked.

"I guess." She started the car and followed the route the truck had taken, but lagging.

"Because of what you said? My uncle and all?"

"Yeah. That, and I love you."

She said it so casually, he didn't seem to be sure he'd heard right. Their eyes met for a moment, and she could see the surprise in his gaze, then she turned back to the road.

Logan seemed stunned. "I don't think you ever said that to me before."

"It was always too hard. I wanted to. Maybe I didn't figure I *needed* to, until now. But . . . looking for you, finding you . . . now I know how important it is. To say it."

He touched her cheek, briefly. "You know that I love you, don't you? . . . God, Max, it's nice to be able to just feel my fingers on your skin . . . Are we all right?"

She glanced at him. "I won't lie to you."

"I won't lie to you either!"

She smiled a little, then returned her eyes to her driving. "I can't say that this business with Seth doesn't still bother me . . ."

"He was your brother. It'll always bother you. It

should always bother you." An edge came into his voice. "Just know, I would never do that to you again."

As good as it had been to hear him say he loved her, hearing this pledge felt even better.

They rode in silence for a while.

Then . . .

"Sounds like you're getting ready for a road trip," he said. "You and Lydecker, going to find your mother?"

She smirked humorlessly. "She could be across town, or on another continent. We have to talk to the colonel . . . and you know Lydecker."

"Reliability is not his middle name . . . And if your mother is halfway across the world?"

"I need to find her."

"I understand. Room for one more?"

Max smiled at him. "I don't know. Let's get you cleaned up, and see if I still can stand being seen with you."

He arched an eyebrow. "Have you seen yourself lately?"

"What's that supposed to mean?"

"That sprinkler system wasn't kind to your hair."

"Is that right? Well, you can take a look at me, after I have a nice long hot bath. I may just sleep until Christmas, then let everything sort itself out."

"This is Christmas, Max."

"So it is."

They rode in silence for a while—a sweet, comfortable silence. Finally, maybe halfway home, with Logan asleep in the passenger seat, she pulled off the road and into the lot of a small roadside motel at the edge of a little town. She checked in, unlocked the room's door, then came out to the car and opened the door on his side. He was lolled back on the seat. She touched his arm.

"Come on," she said.

He awoke slowly. "Where . . . are we?"

"Middle of nowhere. Motel."

He said nothing, getting out of the car cautiously, as if he didn't trust his muscles to work—or the exoskeleton, for that matter.

"You can have a shower or bath," she said, "which I'm gonna do, too . . . but what we really need is rest."

They were to the door now, and she had her arm around his waist, helping him walk inside the motel room.

He allowed her to take her bath, and when she had freshened up, and stood in the open bathroom doorway, using the motel's drier on her hair, she found herself alone. She was just about to get concerned when he stepped back into the room, and explained that he'd just run across the highway to a convenience store, where he'd picked up a few toiletries, including a shaver.

He showered and emerged in twenty minutes, the scruffy beard gone, his shirt off, drying his hair.

"You hungry?" Logan asked. "Or should we just go to bed?"

She was already under the covers.

"I thought you'd never ask," she said, and raised the sheet for him.

Max Allan Collins has earned an unprecedented eleven Private Eye Writers of America "Shamus" nominations for his historical thrillers, winning twice for his Nathan Heller novels, *True Detective* (1983) and *Stolen Away* (1991). In 2002 he was presented the "Herodotus" Lifetime Achievement Award by the Historical Mystery Appreciation Society.

A Mystery Writers of America "Edgar" nominee in both fiction and non-fiction categories, Collins has been hailed as the "Renaissance man of mystery fiction." His credits include five suspense-novel series, film criticism, short fiction, songwriting, trading-card sets, and movie/TV tie-in novels, including *In the Line of Fire*, *Air Force One*, and the *New York Times* best-selling *Saving Private Ryan*. His many books on popular culture include the award-winning *Elvgren: His Life and Art* and *The History of Mystery*, which was nominated for every major mystery award.

His graphic novel, *Road to Perdition*, is the basis of the acclaimed DreamWorks feature film starring Tom Hanks, Paul Newman, and Jude Law, directed by Sam Mendes. He scripted the internationally syndicated comic strip *Dick Tracy* from 1977 to 1993, is cocreator of the comic-book features *Ms. Tree*, *Wild Dog*, and *Mike Danger*, has written the *Batman* comic book and newspaper strip, and several comics mini-series, including *Johnny Dynamite* and *CSI: Crime Scene Investigation*, based on the hit TV series for which he has also written a series of novels and a video game.

As an independent filmmaker in his native Iowa, he wrote and directed the suspense film *Mommy*, starring Patty McCormack, premiering on Lifetime in 1996, and a 1997 sequel, *Mommy's Day*. The recipient of a record six Iowa Motion Picture Awards for screenplays, he wrote *The Expert*, a 1995 HBO World Premiere, and wrote and directed the award-winning documentary *Mike Hammer's Mickey Spillane* (1999) and the innovative *Real Time: Siege at Lucas Street Market* (2000).

Collins lives in Muscatine, Iowa, with his wife, writer Barbara Collins; their son, Nathan, is a computer science major at the University of Iowa.

*Here's the guide no Dark Angel
fan should be without!*

DARK ANGEL:
The Eyes Only Dossier

by Logan Cale
Compiled by D. A. Stern

*November 12, 2021: My name is Logan Cale—
though whoever finds this material will undoubtedly
know me better as Eyes Only. . . . Putting these
documents together in one place poses a big risk—
not just to the corrupt, but to the innocent as well.
Yet the chance that these truths might remain
unspoken is an even bigger risk. People may die, but
the truth must live on.*

All the essential information needed to survive in
the stark future of Dark Angel is here, including
classified documents, photos, maps, articles, and
streaming video transcripts. It's been more than a
decade since a nuclear pulse devastated the East
Coast and plunged the United States into chaos.
This book describes Dark Angel's world in detail,
written by the cyber-rebel "Eyes Only."

Published by Del Rey Books
Available wherever books are sold

The saga of Dark Angel continues!

DARK ANGEL:
Skin Game

Someone is killing normal humans in the fog-enshrouded city of Seattle. But the transgenics who live there have problems of their own. Under siege by the oppressive arm of the police, the transgenics must protect their fledgling colony against a world that eyes them with contempt . . . and will do anything to be rid of them. As the murders escalate, Joshua comes to Max with a dire suspicion: the killer may be one of their own. Now Max and her inner circle must investigate the crimes and stop the bloodshed. But what they discover will shock even the most jaded among them—and expose a sinister agenda that leads to an old, nefarious foe. . . .

Published by Del Rey Books
Available wherever books are sold